Magically Delicious

Magic & Mayhem Book Four

By

Robyn Peterman

What Others Are Saying

"Funny, fast-paced, and filled with laugh-out-loud
dialogue.
Robyn Peterman delivers a sidesplitting, sexy tale of
powerful witches and magical delights.
I devoured Magically Delicious in one sitting!"

~ANN CHARLES
USA Today Bestselling Author of the *Deadwood Humorous
Mystery Series*

Acknowledgements

Writing books is the best job I've ever had. Sitting in my sweatpants, t-shirt, sparkly Uggs and no make-up totally works for me. However, as solitary as the writing process may be, putting a book out is a group effort. There are many wonderful people involved and I'm blessed to have such a brilliant support system.

Rebecca Poole, your covers are perfect and your imagination delights me. Thank you.

Meg Weglarz, you save me from myself constantly with your editing. Thank you.

Donna McDonald, you are my partner in crime, one of my dearest friends and one hell of an author. I'd be in deep doodoo without you. Thank you.

Donna McDonald and JM Madden, you are the best and most honest critique partners a gal could have. I'm grateful for you eagle eyes and good taste. Thank you.

My beta readers; Wanda, Melissa, Susan and Karen, you rock so hard. Thank you.

Wanda, your organization skills keep me from going off the deep end. Thank you.

And my family...thank you for believing in me. I love you more than words could ever express.

And my readers...I do this for you.

Dedication

For Henry and Audrey. I love your names and I love you.

Chapter 1

"I'm so sad we're out of pickles." I sighed as I turned over the empty jar. They'd been delicious dipped in dark melted chocolate. I'd even downed the salty juice, much to the gagging dismay of my dad.

"Zelda, while I understand the diet of a pregnant woman is rather, um... unconventional, don't you think chocolate dipped pickles and mustard slathered jelly doughnuts might be bad for the babies?" Fabio suggested as politely as he could considering he was seconds away from heaving.

"Pretty sure they liked it," I said, sticking my finger in the jar and swiping around for droplets of pickle juice. "Now I think the pizza with pepperoni and Snickers was all kinds of wrong. That one didn't quite agree with me."

"Thank the Goddess," he muttered with a wince.

"So next time I'm going to substitute malted milk balls for the Snickers."

"Wonderful," Fabio choked out, paling considerably. "Maybe we should consult a doctor about this."

"Don't have to," I told him with an arched brow and a wide smile. "I'm the Shifter Wanker around here. What I say about health and wellness goes, and DeeDee my doula says I'm doing great. I say we whip up some deep fried bananas with hot sauce."

Fabio was silent as he digested my newest culinary request. He'd been an outstanding enabler in my mission to keep my growing belly full—until now. Poor Wanda—the best baker in town—had lobbed a pot at my head when I'd requested she bake some jalapeno and anchovy chocolate chunk cookies with turkey gravy to dip them in. However, it was the sushi flavored ice cream that made her throw up her hands and ignore me. That was a week ago. My raccoon Shifter buddy was such a softy, I expected her to come back around any day now.

"Look dad, I know it's a little gross, but if I don't eat, I get cranky. When I get cranky, I start fires and blow stuff up. I do believe sautéed M&M's with blue cheese on crackers is a small price to pay to keep Assjacket, West Virginia on the map."

"A *little gross* is an understatement, Zelda," Fabio argued as he wiggled his fingers and magically removed the empty jar from my hands, replacing it with an apple—a plain apple—with no chocolate sauce or Cheez Whiz to dip it in.

Unacceptable.

"Um... what am I supposed to do with this?" I asked as I cocked back and prepared to bean him in the head with the boring piece of fruit.

"It's an apple. Eat it," he snapped, running his hands through his thick mane of red hair that matched my own. "I'm terrified of what you'll give birth to if you keep consuming crap."

"I'll be having puppies," I shot back. "No one yet has given me solid evidence that this is untrue. Puppies will eat anything—including crap—literal definition intended. So quit your bitchin'."

I took a tentative bite out of the apple to make him happy. It tasted amazing even without maple syrup or salsa—not that I would share that nugget. I still wanted something fried and dipped in whipped cream, but maybe the old warlock had a point. What if my kids—or puppies—came out demanding TV dinners, McDonalds and sugared soda?

I hated it when Fabio made a good argument.

"How about this?" I bargained as I polished off the apple and went for another. "I eat three healthy meals a day and my snacks can be chocolaty, fried, salty and wrong."

"How many snacks are we talking?" he asked warily.

"Um… nine?"

"Four," Fabio shot back.

"Six," I countered. "One before and after each meal."

"Fine," he muttered somewhat mollified by the thought of me swallowing anything that wasn't dipped in lard and deep-fried. "You have a witch's metabolism, so the weight gain isn't an issue. I just worry about your health."

"Fabdudio," I said, harkening back to the days before I called him dad. "I'm truly moved by your concern, but I'm freakin' hungry, and my mouth wants yicky stuff. Not sure what you want me to do here."

"I want you to try, Zelda. All I want you to do is try."

Expelling an enormous amount of air through my pursed lips I created a noise that sounded alarmingly like a fart. I tossed three bags of Oreos, four containers of ice cream, twelve bags of chips and my hidden stash of Goobers and Raisinets into the garbage. It was painful, but my dad beamed so wide, I almost felt proud—almost. Getting rid of my stash was a large price to pay since I'd had big plans to eat a gallon of ice cream covered in barbeque chips for dessert, but Fabio was right. I was eating for three, and I needed to feed my puppies some non-fried, non-pre-packaged stuff that grew out of the earth.

I suffered only a smidge of guilt as I knowingly bypassed the cabinet loaded with Twinkies, Munchos and Ho Hos, but that secret stash was for emergencies. A pregnant girl had to do what a pregnant girl had to do. The safety of those around me was important. I was a loose cannon on a good day. Starving and loaded with strange puppy hormones, I was a magical disaster waiting to happen.

"Happy now?" I asked with brows arched high and my arms crossed over my chest.

"Very," he replied.

"Good. If I can't eat, we have to go do something. I can't sit here in the house and not consume everything in sight."

"How about a little shopping?" Fabio suggested with a gleam in his green eyes.

My disappointment at not being able to eat my own weight in sugar vanished at warp speed. Shopping was my third favorite hobby after eating. My first was the horizontal mambo with the sexiest werewolf alive... my newly acquired mate, Mac.

"I do believe I could carve out a bit of time for that," I squealed. I tore around my new enormous kitchen in Mac's house searching for my Birkin bag and my shoes.

The overpriced yet truly spectacular purse had been a gift from my dad. Fabio was making up for the many years of my life he'd missed by not knowing of my existence. It was excessive, but I was on board. I'd recently turned over a new leaf that precluded me from conjuring up expensive designer duds and accessories—which sucked.

Of course, nine months in the magical pokey for accidentally mowing my dad down with my car had given me a lot of time to think. Well, not really. What it had given me were parole conditions stipulating I could only use my magic for the good of others—a rule I secretly liked. However, I had a reputation to uphold. Being a slightly unbalanced healer witch who didn't give a shit about anything was a full time job. I used to be good at the not giving a shit part, but the furry freaks of Assjacket, West Virginia had weaseled their way into my heart when I wasn't looking. My dad was also a determining factor, but mostly it was Mac. I still had an outstanding handle on the unstable and healing parts, but the rest was more of an act than reality now.

"Where are we going?" I asked, shoving my feet into my fabu Jimmy Choo wedges—another gift from dad—and slinging my bag over my shoulder.

"Your choice—Paris, Milan… Target."

Sweet Goddess on a bender, this was difficult. I loved shopping in Milan. Adored Paris, but the salty soft pretzels with the neon orange, melted cheese dip were right at the stupid entrance of Target. Was this a test? Was Fabio screwing with me? Could I get grounded for this?

Wait a second. I was a thirty year old, knocked-up, mated witch with more power in my pinky than most of my kind. No one was grounding my ass—not even my well-meaning father.

My head said Paris. Crème brûlée with a couple of berries on the top was a far better choice than a processed pretzel with a cheese product that had very little to no dairy in it.

Decisions were hard—not to mention speaking—especially when I was drooling.

"Um… Target has a line of maternity clothes," I suggested weakly, willing myself to block the gooey delicious cheese from my brain. Excess mouth water was not attractive—at all. Plus, it was a dead giveaway to my real motive.

"Darling, you're not even showing yet," Fabio said. He lovingly patted my still flat tummy and kissed me on the head. "I was thinking we could blow a wad at Gucci and then pop into Jimmy Choo."

My groan was pathetic to my own ears. Fabdudio was pure evil. I felt pulled in three thousand and forty-one directions. Shoes or orange-yellow warm-ish cheesy goo?

"I think we should stay in the country and go to Target," I mumbled, brushing some not so imaginary cookie crumbs off of my Alice and Olivia mini dress. "If there were any complications with the pregnancy, it would be better to be closer to home and… "

"You want a pretzel," Fabio accused. He closed his eyes, sighed very audibly and tried not to laugh.

"Yes, by the love of all that's magical," I shouted and stomped my foot. "I want a pretzel."

"Would you be willing to skip the cheese?" he negotiated.

"Not sure I can," I answered honestly with a helpless shrug.

"I feel you," he agreed. "They're quite tasty even though I can't identify what the hell is in the cheese. How about you limit yourself to one?"

"Three," I countered.

"Two and you have yourself a deal," he shot back.

"Done!" I yelled and grabbed his hand before he could change his mind. The nearest Target was three hundred miles away. It was a pleasant day to ride our brooms, but it was broad daylight. Getting shot at while flying over West Virginia for being mistaken for a UFO was not my idea of a good time. Poofing—or *transporting* for a more accurate and mature term—would be safer and faster.

Target, an afternoon with my dad and the soft chewy goodness of two pretzels dipped in unidentifiable gelatinous chemicals.

Win.

Win.

Win.

Chapter 2

"I've gone off carbs," Sassy announced, looking uncomfortably constipated.

"Repeat," I said, staring at her with narrowed eyes. I wasn't sure if she was insane or drunk. No one in their right mind gave up carbs. Being that it was tremendously difficult for a witch to tie one on, I opted for batshit crazy.

"*I said* I am no longer eating *carbs*," she squeaked out and doubled over at the waist.

"I'm sorry. That statement makes no sense to me," I said, pushing my de facto BFF toward the bathroom.

I grabbed a hunk of bread and shoved it in my mouth as I passed the counter to prove my point. The cheesy pretzels from my earlier outing with my dad had been heavenly, but I was hungry again. I had no time for crazy talk from a *sort-of* friend or for her to cop a squat on the rug. That would happen soon enough when I blew out my puppies. A full sized nut job named Sassy was not allowed poop on my floor.

"What are you doing?" she asked, digging her feet in and glancing at me over her shoulder.

"I thought you had to go to the bathroom."

"No, I was having a venereal re-catch-on to my new way of life," she explained, walking back to my couch and making herself far too comfortable.

"You mean… *visceral reaction?*" I asked, closing my eyes and telling myself it would be a bad thing to electrocute her.

Sassy had been my cellmate in the magical pokey for nine horrendous months. When we were released, I expected—and prayed to the Goddess—never to see her again. She liked to steal my clothes, was a magical menace and had boobs bigger than her brain. However nothing in life ever went as planned—at least in my life. So here we were in Assjacket, West Virginia hanging out in Mac's house. Which was my house too now since we'd mated.

I had a house. A beautiful house that I'd inherited from my beloved departed Aunt Hildy. After Mac and I tied the metaphorical Shifter knot with a barbaric ritualistic bite that turned out to be hotter than Hades in July, I'd given the house to my dad. Fabio was Hildy's brother and I felt really good about him having it. There were things I missed about the old house, but Mac's home was beautiful. I just had to adjust. He insisted it was *ours*, but calling it that still felt wonky.

"Yes," she said, looking confused. "That's exactly what I meant… *visceral retraction.*"

Correcting her would get me nowhere fast. Apparently *someone* had a Word of the Day calendar. Deciding it would be mean to ride her for trying to extend her vocabulary—albeit shittily—I focused on her ridiculous new edict.

"Why in the world would you give up carbs?" I asked as I chewed happily on my bread.

Sassy gazed at the hunk in my hand with longing. Kind of the same way she coveted my Birkin bag.

"I'm getting healthy," she explained morosely.

"Ummhmm," I said, watching her contort as I popped the last bit in my mouth. "You clearly don't want to give up carbs. What's going on here?"

"Nothing. I'm setting a good example for Chip, Chad, Chunk and Chutney," she replied, not making any eye contact whatsoever.

Chip, Chad, Chunk and Chutney were the full-grown, gum-smacking chipmunk Shifters who'd recently tried to kill me. However, it wasn't their fault. The boys were being blackmailed by the evil warlock, Bermangoogleshitz. The nasty bastard had been holding Chutney hostage until the idiots repaid a gambling debt. In the end, because of my *new freakin' leaf,* I paid off the debt and they were now working it off as permanent residents of Assjacket.

I forgave them their transgression because they were cute in an inbred redneck kind of way—and I was unfortunately becoming nice. The chipmunks were as dumb as a box of hair and couldn't kill a flea. They were vegetarians. Sassy, in all her altruistic craziness, had adopted the little shits and considered herself an expert on mothering now.

It was painfully wrong.

"Sassy, you've never set a good example for anyone. Ever. Why start now?" I asked with a raised brow. I was trying to figure out if this was somehow a ploy to borrow my Birkin bag, but the pieces of the puzzle didn't even remotely fit.

"Because a good mother sets a healthy eating example for her children," she explained, staring at the palm of her hand.

"How much is he paying you?" I asked calmly. I mentally debated if I would shrink all of my father's clothes, sneak over to his house and put his hand in warm water while he slept, or zap him bald.

"Who?" she asked with wide eyes

"My dad. How much is he paying you to spout the no-carbs bullshit?"

"I have no clue what you're talking about," she lied as she crossed her legs and checked out the bottom of her shoe with great interest. "Eating non-processed, organic vegetables and fruits lowers your chestercall and is good for your barn."

"My *what*?" I asked.

"Um... wait a minute," she replied leaning closer to her foot and squinting. "Chestercall and barn... or maybe it's brain. Shit."

"Show me your foot."

"No."

"Show me your foot and your hand or I'll give your *chestercall* a *venereal re-catch-on*."

"What in the Goddess's name does that even mean?" she shouted, completely bewildered.

"You tell me," I countered as I tore off another hunk of bread and dangled it in her face.

"Great Goddess in a banana hammock," she shrieked, grabbing for the bread and stuffing it in her mouth. "He said he would buy me a Birkin bag just like yours if I started eating healthy and got you to do it too."

"So you wrote all that shit down on your shoe?" I asked, trying not to laugh.

My dad was crafty, but clearly not right in the head if he'd stooped to using Sassy as bait.

"And my hand," she added, holding her palm out.

"Brilliant."

Sassy inhaled the bread and then began frantically opening kitchen cabinets looking for more. I sat back and watched until she got dangerously close to my secret stash. No one was going to lay a finger on my Twinkies and live to tell about it.

"Stop— or you'll be the proud owner of male genitalia," I warned her.

"How many times have I told you I don't speak French?" she shot back as she opened the cabinet hiding my precious booty. "You have Twinkies!"

I watched in abject horror as she downed four without even taking the wrappers off. It wasn't until she went for the Ho Hos that I came to my senses and zapped her ass so hard it left a smoking hole in the butt of her jeans.

Wait. Her jeans looked suspiciously like *my* jeans...

Was she wearing my True Religion jeans? I let my head fall to my chest as I confirmed that she was indeed wearing my favorite jeans. What was happening to me? I was maiming people over Ho Hos? I was decimating my own wardrobe over food that had a shelf life longer than I'd been alive?

"That's going to leave a scar," she shrieked with a mouthful of Ho-Ho. "You don't understand. The entire town has gone off carbs. It's awful. Everyone is a cranky butthole."

"The entire town?" I gasped and sat down unsteadily at the enormous oak kitchen table. Dropping my head to the cool surface with a thud, I realized this was war. Fabdudio was the enemy and he would pay. "How did he do it?"

"Everyone in town owes him money," she explained as she joined me at the table with a family sized bag of Munchos.

"Half of the card playing community in the United States owes him money. *He cheats.* However, I don't understand what owing my dad money has to do with giving up carbs."

It took her a minute and a half of chewing and almost choking on the chips she'd shoved in her cakehole before she was able to speak intelligibly. "He's forgiving all the loans if everyone gives up carbs for nine months so you will too."

I ripped the bag from Sassy's hands and ate the entirety of it while I tried to figure out what my next move should be. Fabio was good, but I was better.

"There are no carbs in town?" I demanded as I generously handed Sassy the bag of chip crumbs.

"Or sugar." She ate the tiny pieces and then licked the bag clean.

My hands lit up like fireworks and Sassy dove under the table for cover. While I rationally knew that my dad was doing this out of love and concern, his method sucked. He didn't understand the needs of a pregnant, starving witch who was possibly carrying wolf puppies.

A slow evil grin pulled at my lips and I yanked Sassy out from her hiding place. "We're witches."

"Duh," she replied.

With an eye roll, I pulled her away from my Ho Hos and seated her back on the couch. We were a good two hundred feet from the chocolaty goodness. If she made a run for them, I was pretty sure I could blast her ass out the window.

"We can just conjure up all the carbs we want," I explained. "No worries."

Sassy's brow wrinkled in deep thought—never a good sign. "No can do."

"Are you serious? You're going to go without cookies for nine months?" I shouted.

"Oh my Goddess," she wailed. "When you say it like that it sounds even worse."

Squatting down in front of her I shoved another hunk of bread in her mouth so I could speak without being interrupted. "We can do this, Sassy. We'll just take long nature walks together and eat doughnuts and cheesy noodles when no one is looking."

"No one will buy us taking long walks together," she pointed out through a mouthful.

She was correct, but I was irrational and pregnant. I was bound to do many out of character things. However, spending all my free time with Sassy would raise eyebrows.

"We'll just secretly meet up and pig out. It'll be fine."

"Your dad warded the area with alarms and little tiny carb-eating fairies will show up if there's so much as a scrap of bread within fifty miles."

I gaped at her and considered removing the bread from her mouth to store away for later, but that was even too gross by my standards. This was going downhill fast, but…

"I call bullshit," I snapped. "I've never heard of carb-eating fairies and my house is loaded with carbs at the moment. If they were in the vicinity, don't you think they'd be partying down in my pantry right now?"

Sassy swallowed her bread and glanced wildly around the room. She got up and searched the area, slipping a few Ho Hos into her pocket when she thought I wasn't looking.

"You think he made the fairy thing up?" she asked, now back in her usual state of confusion.

"Yes. Yes, I do," I said with far more confidence than I felt. Knowing my dad, I couldn't be sure. "And even if he didn't, I could take out a fairy. I popped a buttload of honey badgers who wanted to kill me. I could definitely blow up fairies who are after my Captain Crunch."

"I'm in," Sassy yelled, bounding across the large room and throwing herself at me. "You're brilliant!"

"No. I'm pregnant."

"Same difference," she sang as she danced around the kitchen with joy. "Your kids are so lucky to have you for their mom! I would have killed for a mom like you."

I stood silently and tried to figure out what was wrong with her statement, but I was so muddled with the raging hormones in my body due to getting knocked up by a werewolf that I couldn't find the indignation I was looking for. Something was definitely off here. Was I being a good mom? Wait. I wasn't a mom yet. I still had nine long months before I popped out my litter. I was still just me—albeit a little hungrier than usual.

"Okay," I said, now far less sure of my plan. "We'll start walking tomorrow morning. Deal?"

"Deal. What will you wear?" she asked, excited to cheat the system with me.

"Um… green."

"Green?"

"Yep. Tennis shoes and loose green clothing so we'll be camouflaged by the bushes if we have to hide from carb-eating fairies," I said, feeling an uncomfortable pit growing in my stomach.

"Goddess, you think of everything!" she squealed with delight. "I knew you would be my best friend the minute I saw you in the pokey."

"No you didn't," I shot back with a scowl. "You thought I was a well dressed jackass and I thought you were a busty imbecile."

"Not true," Sassy denied vehemently. "I thought you were a murdering jack-hole who spoke a foreign language. But thankfully times have changed. Now I'd say just a jack-hole who speaks French."

"Well, that's certainly a relief," I said in a voice laced with sarcasm.

"Right?" she agreed in all seriousness. "I'll meet you here in the morning, partner."

On that terrifying note, she pilfered a few more Ho Hos before leaving me with my own discombobulated thoughts. I knew this was a mistake, but my cravings and my brain were working independently of each other. It was a tremendously bad plan, but it was the only one I could think of. Carb eating fairies *had* to be fiction.

It was a risky scheme, but living on the edge was nothing new to me. Pushing my unhealthy strategy to the back of my mind, I hid the remainder of my Ho Hos and Twinkies in the back of the cabinet with the paper towels and napkins. Just in case the tiny, flying, bread eating freaks were real, I needed backup.

The best laid plans of mice and men often go awry... or in my case, witches and Ho Hos.

Chapter 3

"You're gorgeous," Mac said as he tossed the huge salad and then arranged the grilled steaks and asparagus on the platter.

The sun was setting on the horizon and we sat on the wraparound front porch of the rustically beautiful log cabin Mac had built. The wood in the outdoor fireplace crackled and danced and all was right in my world. It was all kinds of sexy to have my man cook for me. It was also a very good thing since everything I cooked was inedible and occasionally sent people sprinting to the bathroom.

I eyed the healthy fare warily, but my mouth was watering. "No bread?" I asked casually.

"Weirdest thing," he replied as he put the food on the table and sat down next to me. "The bakery was out and so was the grocery."

I glanced over at him to figure out if he too was my enemy, but he seemed truly flummoxed by the absence of wheat products. Grinning with relief, I dug into my dinner with gusto.

"I'll try again tomorrow, baby," Mac assured me with a smile that sent tingles of happiness all through my body.

I'd fought like a champion to stay away from the wolf who was made for me. It had taken painful therapy sessions with Roger the porno loving Shifter rabbit—more excruciating for him than me—to figure out my fear of commitment. Ironically, it took my playing Joan Crawford in the now infamous Assjacket community theatre production of *Mommie Dearest* to make me understand I was worthy of being loved.

Baba Yaga, the most powerful of all the witches—and my dad's current gal pal—had come to see the horrifying show. She had been dressed as a Madonna wannabe and had her bevy of boring warlock lackeys in tow, but that wasn't what made me realize I was a lovable witch. Nope.

She also brought my real mother. My mother, the very same woman who'd told me I was worthless while growing up, and had even tried to kill me and steal my healing magic. She was also the woman who'd turned my father into a cat when he realized I existed and wanted to find me. Of course, that ended up being a clusterfuck with a happy ending as he'd become my familiar and I'd mowed him down with a car accidently. Thank the Goddess cats really do have nine lives.

My mother no longer possessed her power because I took it from her. She was now locked up in the same magical pokey where I'd recently vacationed myself. There had been no happy ending for us—no revelation that she loved me. No, what she gave me instead, with the tiniest nod of her head, was the confirmation that she was incapable of loving *anyone*.

It wasn't my fault that my mother didn't love me. She simply didn't have it in her. As sad as it was, the admission had set me free. Just because my mother didn't love me didn't mean I wasn't lovable to others. Hence the mating and subsequent buns in the oven…

"Sassy and I are going to start working out," I told Mac, tearing into the steak and veggies.

24

"I'm sorry? I'm sure I just heard you wrong." Mac paused mid-bite and stared in surprise.

"Um… no," I said weakly with a shrug as I studied my salad with scientific fascination. "I think it would be good um… bonding. You know since Sassy is dating Jeeves and all," I choked out.

Mac handed me a glass of water and continued observing me in silence.

As far as lies went, I thought it was pretty good. Jeeves was Mac's adopted kangaroo Shifter son. He'd found him on the side of the road while visiting Australia long before I'd been born, took the bizarre marsupial under his wing, and raised him as his own.

Sassy and Jeeves were now an appallingly affectionate item and were the proud caretakers of the adopted chipmunks. Yes it was all very strange, but also somehow totally right. The real blessing from the Goddess in this particular case was our currently empty nest. Since Jeeves had increased the size of his family to six, he'd moved out of Mac's house—or rather *our* house.

"That doesn't make much sense," Mac said carefully. He was getting savvy to my hormonal outbursts and was a smart man. Treading lightly he continued. "Why not get some fresh air with Wanda or Simon?"

"Wanda is busy at the diner and she's still a little miffed about the anchovy cookie request. And Simon has started a music school for Assjacket. Skunks are very musically talented," I replied easily. At least that was truthful…

"Interesting."

"Also," I added, now on a roll of sorts. "I think Sassy needs me. Since she played my daughter Christina in the show, she kind-of, sort-of looks up to me now."

Another truth. She needed me to help her break my father's new law and I needed her for the very same reason.

"You want me to run her out of town?" he asked with a mischievous grin, always looking out for my best interests.

"Um... no," I replied with a giggle. "She belongs here—as much as it pains me to admit it. And Jeeves would be devastated."

"This is true," Mac agreed with a shake of his head. "He wants to research his family tree because he has *children* now."

"It's a little alarming to imagine a whole bunch of Jeeveses." I took another steak off the platter and ate it practically whole. "Do you think he even has a family to make a tree?"

"Not that I know of, but I told him I'd help."

"Does that make you feel bad?" I asked as I cut the last steak in two and put half on his plate.

If that wasn't love, I didn't know what love was. I could have totally eaten the steak and everything else on the table. However, I was hoping he'd let me have all the bones. Goddess, I'd become disgusting.

"Why would that make me feel bad?" he questioned as he sliced his half into equal pieces and put a section back on my plate.

"You raised him. You're his dad."

Mac tilted his head and smiled. "I don't worry about that. I'm Jeeves' father—maybe not his biological father—but I was there for everything strange and important in his life. Pretty sure that counts."

"Yep. It counts," I told him. "Is it hard?"

"Is *what* hard?" he asked slowly as a grin pulled at his lips, clearly wondering if it was a trick question.

"*Not* your Bon Jovi," I scolded him with a delighted laugh. "That thing is always hard. I meant is it hard to be a good dad?"

"It saddens me greatly that we're not discussing my Bon Jovi. However, the answer to your question is no. It wasn't and isn't hard at all. Jeeves wasn't exactly easy with his, um… "

"Quirks?" I suggested.

"That's one way to put it," Mac said. "Oddities works too."

"Peculiarities."

"Eccentricities," he added.

"Freakishly weird and unsettling habits," I threw in, starting to get into it.

"Yep," Mac said with a chuckle. "But I love him—bizarre ways and all."

"What if our kids are stranger than Jeeves?"

Mac and I both froze as we considered the ramifications of raising people weirder than Jeeves. Goddess, was that even possible? My breathing grew erratic and the lack of oxygen made me dizzy. Making the babies was all kinds of awesome, but the reality of it all? Not so much.

"We'll love them to the moon and back because they're ours," Mac promised firmly, taking my hands in his. "Are you scared?"

Was I? Hell to the yes, I was scared. I grew up with a mother who didn't want me and an absent father—as in never around—because he didn't know about me. There was a distinct possibility I was going to suck butt as a mother.

"I don't know if I'll be any good at it," I whispered in wide-eyed confession mode. "What if they don't like me?"

Mac leaned in and pressed his forehead to mine. "They'll love you as much as I do. And do you know why?"

"Um... because I'll buy them stuff?" I asked, knowing it was a lame answer, but it was the first thing that came to mind.

"Nope. You don't have to buy them anything. Ever."

"Seriously?" I asked, shocked. I was actually looking forward to that part.

"Well, diapers and food and *stuff* like that would probably be a good idea," he said, trying to suppress his grin. "But our son and daughter will love you because you love them. It's really pretty easy."

I digested the mountain of food I'd just eaten more easily than his words. Was it really that simple? They would love *me* because I loved *them*?

"Have you thought about names?" he asked.

Mac stood up and we both cleared the table. Of course there were no leftovers as I'd eaten everything...

"I've been calling them Lucky and Charm in my head," I admitted with a giggle.

"And would that have any relationship to the cereal?" he inquired with a lopsided grin.

"Possibly," I replied as I held the door open with my butt so he could pass. "However, I have no intention of naming them after a marshmallow breakfast treat, no matter how magically delicious it is."

"Thank the Goddess for that," Mac laughed. "I was thinking of something more meaningful."

"Like what?"

"Maybe Hildy for our daughter and Charles for our son," Mac said, rinsing the dishes and piling them in the sink.

And that's when I stared to cry. The dishes I held fell to the floor with a crash and shattered into tiny pieces. I gasped in dismay at the mess I made and cried harder.

"It was just a suggestion." Mac rushed over and pulled me away from the broken plates and bowls. "We can name them anything you want—even Lucky and Charm. I love the names Lucky and Charm."

"I broke your plates," I whimpered pointing to the pile.

"No, honey. You broke *our* plates," he corrected me.

"And that's supposed to make me feel better?" I shouted as a fresh wave of blubbering ensued.

"No, I just meant… " Mac said, running both of his hands through his hair in bewilderment. "I meant you didn't break *my* plates. I thought that wouldn't make it as bad."

"Don't think. It's not helping."

"Roger that." He stood in the middle of the kitchen looking terrified.

"We don't have to talk about names," Mac offered weakly as I continued to stare.

"Hildy and Charles are beautiful names," I sobbed. I staggered over to a chair and fell into it.

"Then we can name them Hildy and Charles," Mac said looking wildly unsure if that was the correct answer.

"They're awful names though," I blubbered and let my head fall into my hands. "Hildy's real name was Hildegard—which should be outlawed—and a boy with the name Charles will get his ass kicked on the playground."

"Okay," Mac said with a helpless shrug. "We won't name them those awful names."

"But they're *good* names," I wailed. "They're perfectly awful."

"You lost me," Mac said, pacing and trying to get a step ahead in the conversation.

Not possible.

"Do either of those names have nicknames that would make them different?" I asked, wiping my tears and my nose on a throw pillow. "Sorry," I mumbled. "I'll get you a new pillow."

"Zelda, everything in this house including the house is *ours—not mine*. Everything I have is yours."

"So I just wiped my snot on *my* pillow?"

"Apparently," he said with a hopeful grin. "Do you want me to snot on a pillow too, so we're even?"

"Um... no... but thank you." I wiggled my fingers and replaced the pillow.

"Are you okay?" he asked carefully, clearly waiting for another breakdown.

"I think so," I told him. "Do you really like those names?"

"Not sure how to answer that," he said with a grimace, scooping me up in his strong arms and sitting us down on the couch.

"Fair enough. I am a little loose cannon-y at the moment." I cuddled up to him and breathed him in. His scent calmed me and I felt safe and loved.

"Um... what just happened there?" Mac smoothed my wild red hair off my tear-stained face and kissed my forehead.

"Not sure," I admitted, wrinkling my nose. "Something comes over me and I have no choice except to go with it. Earlier it was that my outfit looked cute with my shoes."

Mac wisely stayed silent.

"I'll try harder to get a grip." I wasn't quite sure how to do that, but even I knew I was getting out of control. "Sometimes things like too much pepperoni on the pizza or the color of my fingernail polish sets me off. It's hard to explain, but I promise I'll be better."

"Nope," he disagreed. "You can cry about mini skirts, nail polish, pizza, and names all you want. I'll simply hold you and love you—crazy and all."

"You're a glutton for punishment." I pressed my lips to his and then laid my head on his chest.

"Wrong," he shot back with a happy laugh. "I'm crazy in love with the mother of my children. You do what you gotta do and I'll have your back all the way, baby."

"I love you, Mac."

"I love you more, Zelda."

"Not possible," I murmured as my eyes grew heavy. It had been one long freakin' day.

"So possible," he said softly, carrying me back to *our* bedroom. He tucked me in and then climbed in with me. "Go to sleep, beautiful girl. Sweet dreams."

"You too."

"My dream already came true," he whispered into my hair. "She's in my arms."

"That was pretty cheesy." I giggled and snuggled closer.

"I thought it was pretty damn good," Mac said with a very satisfied chuckle.

I didn't know what I did right in my life to deserve this kind of happiness, but if I thought about it too much, I'd cry again. We'd had enough of my hormonal histrionics this evening.

It was perfect.

And so was he.

Well, perfect for me.

Chapter 4

"What in the ever loving hell?" I grumbled, looking out the window and spying half the town in our front yard.

I pressed my face to the glass and groaned. There had to be at least twenty-five friends and neighbors on the lawn waving at me like idiots—and Sassy was front and center looking wildly confused.

I was dressed for a covert eating mission. Glancing down at my camo pants, olive green t-shirt and kick ass combat boots, I let my chin fall to my chest in defeat. The outfit was a sure sign that something was up. Mac had said nothing about my out of character attire. He was gamely going with whatever weird quirks I'd developed. His raising of Jeeves and all his oddities had been outstanding training for dealing with a magically unbalanced pregnant mate.

How in the Goddess's name were Sassy and I supposed to go for a *walk* if I was hosting an impromptu after-breakfast shindig? This was messed up, and if Sassy had leaked our plan, she was getting a purple Mohawk and a chin wart with a gnarly hair sprouting out of it.

33

"I have a surprise for you," Mac announced from behind me, causing me to whip around and almost blast his ass through the roof.

"Shitballs," I shouted. *"Do not* sneak up on a hungry, knocked up witch. You could lose something important which would suck—for both of us."

Mac's laugh earned him an enormous eye roll.

"We just ate. And if I'm remembering correctly—which I am—you had three veggie omelets, two bananas, a carton of strawberries and a half gallon of orange juice."

"And?" I asked with my hands on my hips and my eyes narrowed to slits.

"And," he said, not quite as jovial. "I'm thinking it might be time for a snack?"

I sighed dramatically and moved away from the window. The excited waving mob was too much to take at 8 AM without any real carbs in my system. Maybe I could text Sassy and sneak out the back door.

Mac rustled around in the kitchen and came back with a Ho Ho as a peace offering. Dangling it provocatively in my face, he made his way to the front door. I followed him like Pavlov's dogs followed Pavlov. It was not pretty, but he had a Ho Ho.

"Here's the deal. You come outside with me. I show you your surprise and then you get the Ho Ho."

I considered the terms for all of three seconds before agreeing. "Give me the Ho Ho and you have yourself a bargain," I told him. I needed to pocket that baby in case my dad was out there. I would smite the bejesus out of anyone who tried to deny me a Ho Ho for my own good—including my sperm donor.

Mac paused and squinted with his head cocked to the side, but handed the booty over without me having to fight him for it. This was a relief since it would be mortifying to brawl over a Ho Ho. I was now positive he was completely unaware of the evil plot against me. This was good since he obviously knew where my secret stash was.

"You wanna explain why sea of Shifters are loitering on our lawn?"

"Nope."

"Okay fine. Then what's the surprise?" I asked as I followed him out to the front porch.

"Well, it wouldn't be a surprise if I told you, pretty girl. Take my hand and close your eyes."

Closing my eyes, I smiled. Mac's surprises were awesome. He'd built me a tree house that I called the Floating Nookie Hut. It was beautiful and one of my favorite places in the world. The meadow surrounding it was magical and I often went alone just to think and eat Twinkies.

The front yard intruders murmured with excitement and I felt a tingle of silly joy in my tummy. As much as I needed some pancakes with hot sauce and whipped cream, the feeling of having real friends around me trumped my cravings.

We walked a few feet then Mac scooped me up in his arms and continued walking. Cheers and laughter from the happy group made my smile widen.

"Can I open my eyes?" I asked, willing myself not to peek.

"Not yet, little witch," he said with a chuckle.

After a brisk five-minute walk with the peanut gallery tagging along, Mac put me down on my feet and kissed the top of my head.

"Open your eyes," he said.

I did. And then I closed them and reopened them a few times to make sure I was seeing what I thought I was seeing. In front of me was a charming log home with a wrap around porch. A few comfortable rocking chairs dotted the porch and an outdoor fireplace flickered and burned. Two large bay windows sparkled in the morning sun and I could see beautiful shabby chic-ish looking curtains inside.

But it was the large sign that made my water works start. *OFFICE OF THE SHIFTER WANKER-walk-ins welcome* was carved into a large wooden sign and propped up on the railing.

I sprinted over with the town on my heels and threw open the front door. There was an adorable waiting room and several rooms set up for patients. Cozy couches and chairs in non-offensive stripes were arranged in a welcoming circle and an official looking receptionist's desk was on the far wall. A magazine rack loaded with Cosmo, Vogue and National Geographic was conveniently situated near the seating area. A coffee and tea station was to the right of the reception desk.

"This is for me?" I whispered to an inordinately proud Mac.

"Yep," he said, pulling me to the back of the cabin with the mob moving right along with us. "And this is your office."

"Oh. My. Goddess," I gasped out. It was entirely done in dark green, cream, gold and peach. The color scheme went perfectly with my red hair. The couch was the most fabulously odd shape and the chair was done in some kind of silky gold brocade. "Is this what I think it is?"

"If you think it's Prada with a little Hermes thrown in, then you're correct," Fabio squealed even more excited than I was.

Dancing around the room with glee, I stopped to kiss Mac soundly and high fived every hand in the room. And then my somewhat uncoordinated gyrating came to an abrupt halt. I really didn't want to terminate my happy dance, but my newly found, and pain in my ass conscience had reared its ugly little head. Something was not right here.

"Wait," I shouted.

Everybody froze, including the few who were still trying to wedge themselves through the door. Fabio quietly tried slip out of the room.

"Not so fast, Fabdudio," I said as I grabbed his hand and yanked him back in. "How exactly was this procured? I wasn't aware any of this was on the market yet."

"What?" Mac questioned, stepping up and giving my sticky fingered father the eyeball.

"I didn't steal it," Fabio protested. "*Exactly.*"

"Define exactly," Mac said, taking the words right out of my mouth.

"Fine," Fabio said with a put upon sigh as he made himself comfortable on the green velvet Prada couch. "It's not on the market *yet*, but it was so perfect for my girl, I had to have it."

"That doesn't answer the question," I pointed out, knowing it would kill me for the furniture to have to go. But go it would if he'd stolen it. The irony here was that my dad was loaded. He didn't need to *lift* anything.

"There are several ways to look at it," Fabio explained as rationally as an irrational warlock with a penchant for helping himself to others' belongings could. "Yes, I took it out of a showroom in Milan. However, I left an enormous wad of cash—at least two times what the retail's rumored to be—and a cryptic, unsigned apology note in its place."

We all pondered that one for a long moment—he did have an argument. It was weak, but...

"This one is tricky," Mac muttered. I could see he was trying not to laugh at the putout yet hopeful expression on my dad's face.

"He did pay for it," Roger the rabbit chimed in. "It's murky, but not definitively illegal."

"I don't gots no problem with it," Fat Bastard, my wiseguy cat grunted as he waddled into the room followed by his equally overweight furry cohorts, Boba Fett and Jango Fett.

All three extended their kitty claws and prepared to sharpen them on my obscenely expensive, questionably acquired couch. Not in this lifetime. I dove at the idiots like an Olympic swimmer going for gold.

"I don't know how many lives you dorkfaces have left," I huffed as I landed on top of them. "But you're about to be one less if you shed on my couch."

"Ease up, Dollface," Fat Bastard grumbled as he crawled out from under the pile. "We was just humbiebuttwashin' you."

"That's right. Not a frumbleasswank scratch or hair on it," Jango concurred indignantly as he lifted his leg and *peed* on my couch.

The crowd went silent and crouched down for cover. I wasn't sure if it was that my cat had just urinated on a fifty thousand dollar couch and they expected my retaliation, or if they thought I'd fry him for calling me a frumbleasswank, whatever the hell that meant. The threesome were forever trying to get new profane catch phrases to take. I was pretty sure the two just uttered had no chance of surviving.

Not a day went by that I didn't consider dropping my familiars off at a pound several hundred miles away. However, it would be useless, as they'd always make their way back to me. We were stuck with each other. Forever. Goddess help me.

"If any of you relieve your bladder on my couch again, I'll fry your asses so crispy, you'll pass for fried chicken," I informed the trio as I stood up far more gracefully than I'd landed.

With a wave of my hands, I cleaned the couch. And for good measure, I produced three cat carriers and locked the little shits in them.

"So are we good?" Fabio inquired, rearranging the throw pillows on my now pee-free couch.

"Zelda?" Mac asked, letting the decision be mine.

Goddess, what was I supposed to do here? A couple of months ago this would have been a no brainer. I'd have kept the dubious booty and loved it with a passion. But now... I was going to be a mom. Pretty sure moms weren't supposed to accept hot upholstery.

"It has to go back," I choked out, gratefully accepting a paper bag from my therapist, Roger.

Breathing into it with enormous gulps of air, I was able to stave off the nausea that had overcome me. The thought of saying goodbye to Prada and Hermes was difficult, possibly as difficult as denying myself Ho Hos.

"That might be a problem," Fabio said, covertly giving my cats an approving nod.

"Why?" Mac asked, noticing the exchange.

"Cuz numbnuts pissed on it," Fat Bastard announced with pride from his cage as Jango raised his paws over his head in victory. "Can't return no piss furniture."

Dysfunctional didn't come close to defining my family.

"He has a point," Wanda said with a twinkle in her eye.

Her adorable son Bo was perched on her hip as she examined the *damaged* couch. My father looked all kinds of guilty and I realized they'd probably planned it.

"Good by me," Bob the beaver stated with his unibrow wrinkled in distress or excitement. I was never quite sure. "At least it was paid for. I say we get on the bus and take Zelda berry picking."

A chorus of yesses rang out and I glanced around in confusion and fear. What the hell was Bob talking about? It was December for Goddess's sake. I had to *work out* with Sassy. Berry picking was not on my agenda unless they were covered in chocolate and had queso to dip them in.

That's when I noticed my dad slipping away and looking mighty proud of himself. This was his idea to keep me away from Ho Hos.

Not happening.

"Um, I hate to burst your bubble," I told everyone as little Bo took my hand and began pulling me along with the exiting group. "Berry season was over a long time ago. There's frost on the ground."

"These are magical berries," Simon assured me with a smile and a quick hug. "Very healthy and delicious. You'll love them."

"How far are we going?" I asked morosely, pissed for letting myself get shoved onto a bus with all my friends.

"It's about fifty or so miles out of town," Mac said, standing in the door of the bus. "Baby, do you mind if I stay here? I've got a few issues I need to follow up on."

I almost shouted with joy, but that would be weird even for me. Fifty miles away from town got me out of range of the magical carb-eating fairies—if they existed. I could get lost with Sassy for thirty minutes or so and down a few hundred thousand calories. Win. Win.

"It's okay. I'm good," I said, grabbing Sassy as she passed and pulling her into the seat next to me.

"Bring me some berries," Mac said, blowing me a kiss and backing off the bus.

"Will do," I promised, returning the air kiss.

Glancing around the bus, I wondered if anyone was onto me. No one seemed to be staring. My dad got into the driver's seat and whistled a little tune as he fired up the bus and headed down the drive. Little did Fabdudio know, I was way smarter than him.

Waaaaaay smarter.

Chapter 5

Simon was correct. The berry patch was indeed magical and was exactly fifty-two point seven miles from town—potentially far enough to be carb-eating fairy free. There were berries of every color imaginable. Juicy bursts of color peeked out from bright green leafy bushes as far as the eye could see.

I was tempted to stick to the fruit, but I was jonesing for pancakes with salsa and whipped cream. Now all I had to do was lose twenty-five Shifters... and one interfering warlock... and I was good to gorge.

"What is this place?" I directed my question to Wanda and Simon as they handed out wicker baskets to the group.

"Don't really know," Simon replied. "It's been here as long as I can remember. Must be glamoured though."

"Why do you say that?" I asked, accepting a basket so I wouldn't reveal my nefarious plan to eat my own weight in carb-y goodness.

"No human has ever stepped foot in the area. Only magicals," Roger explained with his pink nose twitching in the cold air. "It's basically a wrinkle in time."

"Ohhhh, I loved that book," I said.

"No, no, dear, not the book. Although, I adored that one too," Roger said with a smile. "This place *is* a wrinkle. It's not on any map. It doesn't exist."

"Not possible," I countered, skeptically. "There's either a spell on the land or all you guys have been drinking before four in the afternoon."

"Has to be a spell," Fabio said glancing around in appreciation. "I've heard about places like this, but have never come across one before."

"Is it dangerous? Are we in some witch or warlock's territory?" I asked, trying to get a sense of malice in the area.

Fabio paced a large circle and I followed on his heels. The Shifters watched us with curiosity, but very little concern. It was clear they'd been visiting this *wrinkle* for many years and had no problems.

"I sense something, but I don't think it's evil." Fabio shrugged but continued to scan the horizon.

"Are the berries poisonous?" I examined a bush loaded down with plump orange and purple berries. They looked delicious, but I'd learned the hard way that looks could be wildly deceiving.

"They're fine," Wanda assured my dad and me. "We'd all be dead as doornails of they were lethal. I've been baking with these babies for decades."

"And will you be baking with what you gather today?" I asked, giving my dad the stink eye.

He was conveniently examining his nails.

"Well… " Wanda hesitated, and if I wasn't mistaken rolled her eyes a smidge. "I'm working on a new crust made with only almonds and honey. So yes, I'm going to give it a shot."

A shudder of happiness skittered through me. Maybe there was a way around the no carb rule after all. I could get on board with honey and almond crust as long as I had a bottle of hot sauce and maybe some guacamole to put on top.

"Okay people," Roger, my porno-loving therapist called out, hopping up and down and looking more like a rabbit than he did when shifted. "Stay in groups of two or three and meet back here in an hour. Bob, please don't eat the yellow berries. They don't agree with you and I refuse to be asphyxiated on the bus ride home. Again."

"There's something to look forward to," I muttered and said a quick prayer to the Goddess that Bob followed the rules.

Bob gave a weak thumbs up and slunk off into the berry patch with a few other beavers. His lack of vocal assurance didn't bode well for a fart free ride back. I could always whip up some nose plugs for my neighbors. While some might argue that I'd be using my magic for self-serving purposes, I'd maintain my innocence in that I was defending my people against a deadly gastric invasion. However, Bob—if guilty—would not be receiving any olfactory assistance.

My sense of smell had increased tenfold with my pregnancy. Bob the beaver could lose more than just friends if he had a tooting issue in an enclosed space with me. I was curious what the berries tasted like, but vowed to avoid the yellow ones as well. I was far too polite to suffocate my friends.

"Ididntgetabaskethowdoicarrymyberrieswithoutabask et?" Chunk the gum-smacking, marble mouthed chipmunk Shifter fretted, running around in circles and pulling on his shock of wiry hair.

While the entire group from Assjacket tried to figure out what in the hell he'd just said, I waved my hand and produced a few more baskets for those who didn't get one. I even kept the price point down. In the old days, I would have conjured up a Longaberger. However, since Chunk was notorious for losing and/or destroying things, I went for something sturdy, simple and cheap.

"Here you go," I said handing the little weirdo his basket and giving him a quick hug.

"Thankyouoshifterwankeralmighty," he said with a respectful bow.

"Dude, drop the almighty part. While I do enjoy a nice ass-kissing as much as the next witch, pissing off the Goddess is not my idea of fun. She can be a gaping butthole extraordinaire."

"Duck," Fabio shouted as a zap of purple lightning hurtled down from the clouds aimed at my ass.

"Motherhumpinshitmonsters," I screeched, grabbing Sassy's water bottle and dousing my smoldering butt.

The crowd dispersed like confetti from a clown cannon as I took my stinging punishment with a few new swear words and the real need to lift my middle finger at the sky.

I refrained. One massive ass zapping was enough for me.

"Zelda, darling," Fabio said, trying not to grin. "Are you all right?"

"Fine," I grumbled through clenched teeth as the Shifters peeked out from beneath bushes and a couple from branches in the trees. "Everything is fine here. You all can just go about your business. Nothing to look at except a hole in my pants."

"Your balls are ginormous," Sassy congratulated me.

"Pretty sure I might have just lost one in that transaction," I said, rubbing my butt.

"Do you think it was the gaping part or the butthole part?" Sassy questioned as she very creatively pulled us in a different direction than the rest of the group.

"I'm gonna go with that it was the combination of the two," I told her, watching with relief as my dad wandered off in a trio with Simon and his sweet gal pal, Meg.

"We have an hour," I whispered when I was sure we were out of earshot. "Let's walk this way for about ten minutes and then get down to business."

"Did you bring Ho Hos?" she whispered.

"Nope," I lied, feeling for the precious chocolaty surprise in my pocket. "We're gonna conjure up our feast."

She skipped ahead and darted in and out of bushes. I picked a few berries and popped them in my mouth as I watched her do an awkward cartwheel and bash into a tree. She let out a yelp and then slapped her hand over her mouth. Shaking my head, I lambasted myself for bringing her in as my partner in crime. Sassy and her *Sassy ways* were gonna get us so busted.

"Enough with the Cirque de Soleil," I snapped. "If you break something, I have to heal you and then we have less time to eat. That will make me unhappy and I like to blow shit up when I'm unhappy. Are we on the same page?"

"Of what?" she asked.

"What?"

"That's what I just asked," she replied, annoyed.

"You lost me."

"Well, what page are you on? Ten? Seven? Two hundred and three? How can I know if I'm on the same page of I don't know what page you're on?"

"It was a figure of speech," I ground out.

"You really need to stop showing off your multi lingual-ness," she complained with an eye roll and a huff. "Some of us only speak English."

Shoving my hands into my pockets so I didn't zap her toothless, I held on to my sanity by a thread. I had to lose her or she was going to lose something important—like her eyebrows. What had seemed like a brilliant idea in theory was turning out to be a disaster in practice.

I was about to do something that I might regret as I had a limited supply of Ho Hos, but it was the right thing to do if I was going to ditch her.

"Sassy, I'm pretty sure a left my magical food wand on the bus."

"You have a magical food wand?" she shouted as her eyes narrowed dangerously. "Why in the hell don't I have a magic food wand?"

"Um... because you only receive a magic food wand when you're pregnant," I explained, hoping she'd buy the crap I was selling.

Fortunately, she did. Hook line and sinker.

"I knew that," she said, nodding like a bobble head. "We all receive different wands for different needs."

I nodded carefully. We didn't need wands at all. Witches only used them for show or if we were bored. Brooms were the same. We flew without the aid of anything physical. I was pretty sure most of the props came from fairy tales. All of our magic was innate and within our bodies—a gift from the Goddess.

"I have a magical orgasm wand," she confided in a delighted whisper.

"That's called a vibrator."

"Your point?" she demanded, slapping her hands on her hips and raising a brow. The very same brow she was seconds away from losing.

"My point is I need the magical food wand. How about I give you a Ho Ho and you go get it then come back here?"

"A Ho Ho?"

"Yep," I said, withdrawing it from my pocket and dangling it in her face the very same way Mac had done with me.

"I'd give up my left boob for a Ho Ho," she confided seriously. "And it's the slightly bigger one."

With a wince of horror at what she'd just overshared and what I was about to give up, I handed over the Ho Ho. "You can keep your slightly larger mammary. Just go back to the bus and get the wand."

"What if I can't find you?"

"Then just eat the Ho Ho and I'll meet you in an hour."

"Works for me," she said as she skipped off, narrowly missing a low hanging branch.

I watched her until she was out of sight and made a run for some better cover. Meeting up with a Shifter or Goddess forbid, a carb-eating fairy was not on my schedule.

Pancakes and cheese covered Milky Ways were.

Chapter 6

Instead of running, I decided to fly. The scenery below was breathtaking. It was not December here at all. The temperature was a balmy seventy degrees and the plant life exploded in glorious harmony with the Earth. Whoever did this was extremely powerful and very finely attuned with nature.

Touching my still flat stomach, I sighed and grinned. It amazed me to no end that I had two tiny babies inside me. While the thought still terrified me, my joy was starting to push my fear aside. Nothing seemed quite real yet, but I knew it was happening.

"Hi guys," I whispered with a carefree giggle. "Are you hungry? Mommy has some big plans today."

Of course there was no answer. I would have dropped out of the sky if they'd replied, but it was fun to talk to Lucky and Charm.

"Pancakes, beef flavored ice cream, and tacos with whipped cream, here we come!"

Wait.

I froze and hung mid air. Guilt overwhelmed me and I wanted to cry. Nothing unusual about that as of late, but this was different.

I felt horrible. Frustratingly, my dad was right about my eating habits.

And to make matters uglier, I'd lied to Mac about *working out* with Sassy—totally unacceptable. Mac was my mate and the father of my unborn canines. There was no way I was going to jeopardize my happiness with the wolf of my dreams over Ho Hos.

I *was* putting crap in my body. I *was* feeding Lucky and Charm food equally as unhealthy as their namesake cereal. What the hell was wrong with me? Was I so selfish that I was poisoning my babies?

Was I as awful as my own mother?

Floating down to the ground and seating myself next to a bush loaded down with rainbow colored berries, I pondered my predicament. I popped a few in my mouth and went to work on a new plan. Damn, but the berries were tasty.

Breakfast had been good this morning. While I did miss pancakes and toast with ketchup and mustard, I didn't feel the need to behead anyone after my high protein, heavy veggie and fruit morning meal. If Wanda really could make a healthy crust, I could still eat sweets. They might not hold up to the sterling flavor of a Twinkie slathered in pizza sauce, but I'd be able to sleep at night knowing I was being a good mom.

"Little dudes," I said, touching my stomach. "I'm so sorry about the last few weeks. There's a new sheriff in town and she's gonna eat stuff that would make Dr. Spock proud. You in?"

A warm cozy tingle in my tummy made me gasp. As much as I knew my babies—or puppies—were alive inside me, it was the first time I'd felt their presence. With renewed determination to shun Ho Hos, Twinkies, and all things chemical, I stood up and tried to get a sense of where in the hell I actually was.

"I think we might be a little lost," I told my stomach. "Mommy's epiphany made me lose track of where I was flying."

And that's when I saw something strange.

It was tiny and as colorful as the berries, but it was definitely not a berry. Berries didn't have wings and didn't giggle like deranged maniacs. Berries didn't have pieces of cookies in their hands because berries didn't have hands.

Shitballs. Maybe the odometer on the bus was wrong. Maybe we weren't over fifty miles out of Assjacket.

Or maybe the carb-eating fairies followed us.

Or maybe I'd lost my ever-loving mind.

Nope. The high-pitched giggling was real and slightly disturbing. Maybe the fairies had created the berry patch.

"Um, hi," I called out, ready to pop the shit out of the little turds if they were violent. I had much more to protect and live for now. "I'm Zeldo... umannawanna. Show yourselves."

I winced inwardly and almost laughed aloud at my pathetic butchering of my own name, but I had decided mid-sentence not to reveal my real identity to the tiny flying freaks.

There were five of them and they all spoke at once in a language I had no hope of understanding. Thankfully, they seemed pleased to meet me and I did hear them try and wrap their tiny tongues around Zeldoumannawanna. It was all kinds of not going to work...

"Is this your territory?" I asked.

They flitted around in circles with their tiny noses wrinkled in confusion. Clearly they didn't understand my language anymore than I understood theirs. I briefly wondered if they'd understand Chunk. Goddess knew most people couldn't. However, what I did understand was their frantic waving and pointing. They beckoned me to follow.

What to do…

Were they leading me back to the bus or were they leading me into some sort of trouble? Only one way to find out. They were tiny and I knew I could eliminate them, but they'd given me no reason thus far. The cookies they held were more appealing than they were, but I was off of that shit. No more cookies for me.

Grabbing a few berries so I didn't lunge for their cookies, I followed the little carb eaters deeper into the berry patch. Pausing for a moment, I closed my eyes and let the Goddess guide my instincts. I detected no malice whatsoever… and now I was curious.

***

"What the hey-hey?" I squealed with delight out as we came to a clearing and my eyes landed on a life sized gingerbread house—made of *real gingerbread*.

Not only was it made of gingerbread, the adorable small cottage had a wildly colorful gumdrop roof and thick white icing for windowsills. The pink tinted widows were surely made of spun cotton candy and there was a chocolate pretzel gate. It was every pregnant witch's dream come true—or at least it was mine. It just needed some hot sauce and it would be perfection.

The fairies dove on the house and began nibbling away. I carefully opened the yummy gate and walked toward the eighth wonder of the world. It took every bit of willpower I had not to rip off the gate and cram it in my mouth.

"Is this your house?" I called out to the fairies, who ignored me as if I wasn't there.

They were voracious eaters with sharp little teeth, but since their mouths were so tiny they barely made a dent in the house. As awestruck as I was, I was also cognizant that cute gingerbread houses usually came with evil witches... at least according to fairy tales.

Again, only one way to find out.

I knocked tentatively at the door that I discovered was made out of chocolate. I might have licked my knuckles a few times. And I might have knocked longer than necessary, but it was chocolate and I wasn't made of steel.

"Anybody home?" I asked, continuing to knock—and lick.

The carb-eating fairies were worthless. Not being able to understand their odd chattering didn't help, but they didn't even hang around to meet the owner. They'd eaten and then flew away when I started to knock. It was just the edible house and me.

Shit.

"One bite, Zelda," I instructed myself sternly. "Just one small bite. It's somebody's home, for Goddess's sake. You can't eat someone's shelter no matter what it's made of."

Who would know? Clearly the owner wasn't home. What kind of idiot built their house out of cookies and candy and expected it not to get eaten? Honestly, I would have preferred sour cream and onion chips with a few grande burritos thrown in, but the gingerbread was still working for me.

Carefully peeling off a small corner of the door and dipping ever so lightly in the windowsill, I ate it. Sweet Goddess on a spaceship headed straight to Hell, it was the best chocolate and vanilla icing I'd ever tasted.

"Just one more little corner," I promised myself aloud as if actually speaking the words would make me stick to the plan.

It wasn't until I came up for air that I realized I'd consumed the entire door, part of the windowsill and about a third of the chimney.

"Fuck," I muttered, feeling awful. My self-control was nonexistent. What kind of mother was I going to be if I wasn't able to stop myself from eating people's houses?

"I'm an awful mother. I suck. I don't deserve my puppies. Sassy is a better mother than I am. Well, not really," I mumbled, realizing my self-flagellation had gone a bit too far—but only the Sassy part. The rest was sadly true.

"You like my house, chickie?" a fairly neutral female voice asked from behind me.

"Shitshitshit," I croaked as I turned and tried to position my body so the lady wouldn't realize I'd polished off her door. The gnawed on chimney was impossible to hide. Goddess, I couldn't even recall eating the damn chimney.

"You have chocolate on your chin," the woman said.

She stood about five feet tall, had steel gray hair and vivid green eyes. She was definitely a witch, but she'd aged for some odd reason. I'd never heard of an old witch. Well, not true. There were tons of old witches, they just didn't *look* old. We stopped aging around thirty-ish.

"I am so sorry," I blustered wondering if I should get down on my knees. I'd just eaten a good portion of her house. I was sure an apology wasn't going to cut it.

Wiping the chocolate off my chin, I awkwardly tried to smooth out the gaping icing holes that use to be a charming windowsill.

"Don't know whether to zap your ass or thank you. I've grown tired of the chocolate door. Was thinking of changing it to caramel," she said as she wiggled her nose and produced a three-foot long candy cane. Holding it in her gnarled hand she used it as a walking aid and moved closer to me.

"Honestly, I've had one hideous butt zapping today from the Goddess—which sucked ass. Pun intended. Maybe we could work out another form of retribution," I suggested with a hopeful smile.

She tilted her head, stared at me for a long moment and then touched my hair.

"Is that your real color, girlie?" she questioned as she stepped by me and entered her door-less house.

"Um, yes. And I have a name," I told her, knowing she'd probably need it to report me to Baba Yaga. I hung my head in shame and imagined spending more time in the magical pokey for this one.

"Yep, I heard it. Zeldoumannawanna. Worst name I've heard in all my years. Your mother must have hated you to saddle you with that one."

I almost laughed at the irony of her nailing my relationship with my mother on the head, but thought better of it. It wouldn't do to have her think I was amused at my horrible transgression of inhaling a good portion of her home. She could still give me a very deserved ass zapping.

"She did hate me, but that's another story altogether. I really am sorry about eating your house. See, I'm pregnant with twin puppies, and your house is made out of cookies. Not that that's an excuse," I added hastily and then tried to peek over her bony shoulder. "Can I ask you a question?"

The woman raised her eyebrows, crossed her arms over her chest and waited. I took that as a yes.

"What's your furniture made out of?"

"Wouldn't you like to know," she replied with a cackle. "I've decided not to zap your sorry butt because you amuse me. However, you will return here for the next few days and help me re-bake my house."

"Can't we just do a little hoodoo and fix it up?" I asked.

It wasn't that I didn't want to come back and help her. It's just that I'd have a difficult time explaining this one to Mac—and my dad—and my friends.

"Magic does not solve everything, girlie," the woman snapped harshly. "Magic is a gift to be used wisely, not to get an irresponsible witch out of doing the right thing."

She had me there. Crap.

Rocking back and forth on my feet, I tried to think of a gracious way out of it. There was no gracious way out of it. She was actually being pretty damn nice about the fact I ate her house. It was the least I could do to help her re-bake it. However, there were a few problems.

"Three things," I said wanting to be up front and lay all my crappy cards on the table. "I can't cook at all—truly, not at all. My familiars will eat cardboard and they can't even smell my cooking without getting ill. Secondly, I'm on a carb and sugar free diet. Third, I have no freakin' idea where I am at the moment so getting back here could be an issue."

"One, you'll learn to bake. Two, you could have fooled me with your diet since my door and chimney are missing. Three, you've been here so you can poof back anytime you want. Just picture it in your pea brain."

I nodded as politely as possible, swallowing back the retort that was on the tip of my tongue. I was getting off fairly easy here. My smart mouth could set me back. "What time should I come tomorrow?"

"Noon. Swear on witch's honor that you'll return," she insisted, making me very uncomfortable. However, I was in the wrong here, and she had every right by magical law to demand punishment.

"I give you my word on witch's honor," I told her.

She nodded curtly as if satisfied. And then waved her hands.

I thought she was waving goodbye.

I was terribly mistaken.

A fierce wind that smelled like fresh from the oven, just baked cookies whipped me up and hurtled me through the air like a rag doll. The little old witch's power was so intense, I didn't have a second to counteract it. Goddess, I never even saw the mini-tornado coming.

Dying for eating a house seemed a little harsh. If I'd just stuck to my new healthy eating plan though, none of this would have happened.

Trapped in a kaleidoscope of swirling color I cursed the lying little witch. She told me I could re-bake her damn house. Never, never, never trust anyone with an edible house. They were all fucking crazy.

I landed with a thud right in front of the bus much to the shocked surprise of my friends. In my hand was a basket filled to the brim with rainbow colored berries and not a hair was out of place on my head. I was both incredibly confused and grateful to the nut job with the cookie house. However, a heads up that the old bag wasn't sending me to the Next Adventure would have been nice.

"Holy shit," Sassy shouted, checking out my basket of unusual fruit. "Where did you pick those?"

"Um... on the trail," I lied as everyone admired my find.

"Never seen these before," Wanda said as she popped one in her mouth and groaned with pleasure. "Oh my! These are heavenly."

"How about I come back tomorrow… or everyday this week and try to find them again?" I suggested.

It was lame, but it would get me out of having to hide my coming back.

"We'll all come back!" Roger announced to an agreeable crowd.

"Yes," Fabio agreed, clearly thinking it would keep me away from carbs. "Outstanding idea."

Little did he know…

However, if the old witch was dangerous, I didn't want anyone I cared for getting hurt. I'd eaten the house all by my lonesome. I was going to have to repair it the same way. If I shared my predicament, they'd all want to help.

Shit.

"How about four tomorrow afternoon?" I suggested casually, praying to the Goddess they'd go for it. It gave me the time to poof over and bake with the cray-cray witch, poof back home, and then take the bus out with my people.

"Four it is," Fabio shouted joyously, giving me a loving, pride-filled glance.

Feeling lower than low for lying to my dad and everyone else, I slunk onto the bus. *Of course* Bob ate the yellow berries and I was yet again the champion for whipping up nose plugs. I even gave Bob one. He didn't deserve it, but I needed something to make me feel like a good person.

Saving my friends from asphyxiation would have to suffice for today.

Chapter 7

"I need you to get rid of the Ho Hos and Twinkies—all of them," I told Mac firmly, as I held onto the edge of the kitchen counter for purchase. I desperately wanted to tell him I'd eaten a house, but decided I'd save that for another time. He'd get all overprotective if he knew I was going back to re-bake what I'd chowed down on.

Mac went ashen and backed away from me. "That's a little drastic."

"Yes," I agreed, squeezing my eyes shut so I wouldn't see him do the deed. "I'm turning over a new leaf."

"I thought you already did that," Mac replied easily, but I could detect the panic in his voice.

"I did, but this leaf isn't for me. It's for Lucky and Charm. I'm no longer going to put bad things in my body. Of course after I blow the kids out, I'll go on a Twinkie-Ho Ho binge that will make the Guinness Book of World Records."

"Your way with words never ceases to amaze and appall," Mac said with a chuckle, gathering me into his arms. "You can eat a Ho Ho every now and then as long as it's not all you're eating."

His reasoning was sound, but I knew myself far better than he did. There was no stopping me at one Ho Ho—not while I was knocked up. Hiding the Ho Hos was the only way to go—not just hiding. I'd find them if they were hidden. They needed to be destroyed.

"How about this? Why don't you eat them and then we can go parking and make out like teenagers. I'll be able to taste them and making out leads to sex. It's a win win for everyone," I suggested hopefully.

"I like it, but I hate Ho Hos," Mac replied as he went to the secret stash cabinet and removed the over processed, chemical ridden, manna from Heaven.

"How in the Goddess's name does anyone hate Ho Hos?" I demanded so shocked by his admission, I didn't realize he was putting the sweets down the running disposal.

"I don't know." He shrugged and grinned. "I don't like them."

"Wait," I shouted as he went to put the last Ho Ho into the disposal. "Does your Bon Jovi like Ho Hos?"

A slow sexy smile spread across Mac's lips as he tucked the lone roll of chocolaty delight into his shirt pocket. "My Bon Jovi *loves* Ho Hos."

"Excellent," I squealed as everything south of my bellybutton went into overdrive. "Get the motorcycle fired up. We're going to the Floating Nookie Hut."

"The what?" Mac asked, pinching the bridge of his nose and trying not to laugh.

"My tree house that you built for me," I explained as I threw a bunch of props into a large shopping bag so we could play the x-rated version of *The Little Mermaid* or *Sleeping Beauty*. "I named it."

"Of course you did," he replied with a shake of his head and a chuckle. "Meet you in three."

Mac sprinted out the front door with werewolf speed and I heard the motorcycle roar to life. The Bon Jovi Ho Ho was the last Ho Ho I'd have until Lucky and Charm were born. I was going to make that Ho Ho last a very long time. Mac was going to learn to *love* Ho Hos tonight.

And I was going to *love* teaching him.

***

"Holy hell," Mac shouted on a gasp as I finished him and the Ho Ho off with great pomp and circumstance. "Are you sure you're off Ho Hos for nine months?"

"Yep," I replied with a very satisfied grin. That had been a total win. I got my Ho Ho and Mac got the blowjob of the century.

"Damn," he said as he slid me up his sexy, muscled and very naked bod. "I suppose we can find other ways to have fun."

His eyes were hooded and I giggled as I felt his Bon Jovi come back to life with his suggestion.

"You're an animal," I said, wiggling and getting as close as I could. Crawling inside him wouldn't be close enough.

"Your point?" he shot back with a grin that set my girlie parts on fire.

"No point," I said, straddling the most beautiful man in the world. "Just an observation."

"Would you like to do more than observe?" he inquired, lifting my hips and placing me over his very happy camper.

"I could get on board with that," I purred as I lowered myself and buried him inside my body.

Pressing my forehead to his, I tried to keep my breathing steady. We fit together perfectly and it only got better and better each time.

"How did this happen?" I whispered as I began to rock back and forth loving the feel of his body stretching mine.

"Well, I put my Bon Jovi in your Little Red Riding Hood and then... " he started explaining clinically with a shit eating grin on his face.

"You're a dork," I said and then gasped as he raised his hips causing little stars to rip across my vision.

"I'm *your* dork," he growled, pressing his mouth to mine and nipping at my bottom lip. "I'm your mate and the father of our children. And you are *mine*."

"Goddess, that's so hot," I cried out as everything started to get serious.

Flipping me to my back while still buried deep inside me, Mac's sapphire blue eyes sparkled with lust and his fangs dropped. Never in my thirty years did I think I would find pointy teeth sexy, but Mac could make madras pants and a Peter Pan collar appealing. My wolf was hotter than the middle of August in Hell. And he was all mine.

"I love you," he said while slowly and very methodically moving in and out of my very willing and needy body.

"I love you more," I whispered, cupping his beautiful face in my hands. "Did you know as the pregnancy progresses I'm going to get hornier?"

His whoop of joy made me giggle. His lips crushed mine and his leisurely movement was leisurely no more. He was all business now and I was all in. Unable to hold back my pure joy, my magic swirled around us. Glistening rose colored bubbles bounced around the room and a sparkling golden breeze caressed our overheated bodies.

As the speed of our love making increased, all rational though ceased as I joyfully met each powerful thrust. Mini orgasms took the express train through my writhing body as his fangs scraped the very same spot he'd claimed me.

Pulling his thick dark hair I tried to tell him what I needed without words. Words were impossible since all that was coming out me were moans, pants and delighted screams.

"What do you want, sexy girl?" he asked hoarsely. His eyes were unfocused and he was holding on by a thread.

He hadn't bitten me since our mating. I was very aware that he'd wanted to on several occasions, but I'd avoided it. The one and only time he done it we broke the bed and I got knocked up. I was still a little scared of getting knocked up again.

Wait. What the hell was I thinking? I knew my brain was addled with hormones and the fact that I was orgasming repeatedly at the moment, but surely I wasn't *losing* brain cells. My reasoning made no sense whatsoever. I was already knocked up. I was fairly sure I couldn't get any more knocked up than I already was. However, he was a wolf and I was a witch. Were there different rules here?

Shit.

"I want you to bite me, but only if you can guarantee that I won't end up with anymore buns in the oven than I already have," I gasped out, rolling my hips and arching my body toward his.

"Um... what?" he asked trying not to laugh.

"If you so much as chuckle, your Bon Jovi will be singing the blues—as in the very painful blue ball blues," I hissed. I was mad and embarrassed, but my writhing body wasn't clued in as it gripped him like a vise within me.

"No, baby," Mac assured me. "You have all the buns in the oven you're going to have this time."

"What do you mean *this time*?" I demanded, wrapping my legs around his waist as a delicious tingling started low in my belly.

"I mean *this time*," he said, lowering his sharp sexy fangs to my neck.

I wasn't quite done chewing on the *this time* comment, but it could wait. I needed to see how much I liked Lucky and Charm before I agreed to The Captain and Crunch. Honestly, I was already wildly in love with my tiny marshmallow treats, but two might be enough. There was no telling how much therapy I'd have to pay for if I had four. I knew I'd screw them up one way or another, but it would be because I loved them too much.

The pop of my skin should have freaked me out, but all it did was send me over the edge. However, the fall was yet to come.

And then my world tilted on its axis. Mac's bite turned my words into babble-ville. I wasn't even sure what I was screaming. Glitter and bubbles filled the room. My body jerked and shuddered as Mac's did the same.

The sounds coming from deep in his chest spurred on another more intense orgasm and I was pretty sure I heard the bed frame crack. It was all kinds of awesome—way better than Ho Hos.

"You know if we did this all the time, I wouldn't even think about Ho Hos," I said still trying to catch my breath as I floated back to reality.

"I like the way you think," Mac replied, tracing my collarbone with his finger and planting little kisses all over my face. "However, it could get a bit awkward if we disappeared into the Floating Nookie Hut for nine months."

"I see your point. Maybe when I have a really bad craving we can have a code word for *I need to get laid now*," I told him with a silly grin.

"And what would this code word be?"

I thought hard for a moment as I breathed in his clean soapy scent and snuggled closer.

"Ho Ho," I replied. "The code word for *do me now* is Ho Ho."

"Works for me. I actually am kind of hungry," he informed me with a panty melting half smirk.

"Would you like a *Ho Ho*?" I asked suggestively, yet kind of alarmed that I was ready to go again.

"I would love a *Ho Ho*."

So we had some more Ho Hos.

And it rocked.

It rocked the bed completely in half and it rocked a mysterious hole in the wall.

Ho Hos were deliciously destructive.

Chapter 8

"What's going on?" I asked, staring in dismay at our magical meadow that appeared to be wilting in the early morning sun.

We'd slept on our *broken for the second time* bed and awoke at dawn's butt crack. Mac was an early riser and the birds that shared the tree with the Nookie Hut were freakin' loud. As it was December there were no flowers, but the thick dark green pines looked sad and droopy.

"This is what I've been looking into," Mac said, fingering the sagging pine needles.

He took my hand and led me to the pond usually filled with brightly colored fish—it was dark and murky.

"Can't you get in touch with the Earth?" I asked, concerned.

Mac was so much more than a werewolf Shifter. He was the King of his people and the Goddess had blessed him with an affinity for the Earth. Power like that in a mere Shifter was unheard of, but my wolf was no mere Shifter.

"I've tried," he said, running his hand through his hair in frustration. "It comes back to life for a bit and then disappears."

"Should I cry?" I asked. "Lucky and Charm camping out in my tummy make me an emotional lose cannon."

Mac was a very smart man. I'd left myself wide open with the prior statement. *Emotional Loose Cannon* should be my middle name—pregnant or not. However, my question was legit. My tears caused it to rain in our secret meadow. With Mac's gift and my tears the meadow had come to life in the way it was meant to. But now… not so much.

"No, baby," he said. "The balance in the entire area is off."

"Explain."

"You know Main Street is glamoured to look like a dump," Mac said, leading me to where we'd parked the motorcycle.

I nodded. Humans drove right through Assjacket without a backward glance. This suited the Shifters just fine. Inside the dilapidated buildings, everything was pure enchantment. Everything from the Assjacket Diner to my therapist Roger the rabbit's office was charming and lovely behind the broken down exteriors. The town was one massive sleight of hand, so to speak. It was a testament to the brilliance of my friends since the Shifters lived a very public yet secret life.

"It's falling apart. Buildings are coming down as fast as we rebuild."

"What? I was in town last week," I told him.

"It started two days ago. Can't figure out what the hell is happening," he replied, putting a helmet on my head.

"Take me to town. I'm gonna fix this shit."

***

"It's just a mess," Bob fretted, pulling on his unibrow.

I was hoping Bob had gotten all the yellow berries out of his system but I conjured up a few nose plugs to be safe and tucked them in my pocket. However, the beaver was correct. Main Street was in total disarray.

"Has anything like this ever happened?" I asked, examining the fallen gutters and the crumbling walls of the grocery.

"No," Wanda answered. She shook her head and tried to nail a sideboard back on the store with very little success.

"Very unusual and highly suspect," DeeDee the deer Shifter said while shaking her head, taking my pulse and then measuring my stomach.

Normally, I'd think her bizarre behavior was obnoxious and I'd deck her, but she was my doula and I let her do anything she wanted. She'd helped bring thirty-nine Shifters babies into the world. It was definitely not the doctor behavior I'd seen on TV, but my brand of healing was fairly left of center as well.

"There's a distinct absence of magic here," Fabio observed, perplexed. "Can you feel it Zelda?"

I nodded and shivered. It was the most unusual sensation I'd ever experienced.

"Everybody stand back," I told the gathering crowd. "I'm gonna wing this one."

"Sweet Mother of the Goddess, RUN!" Roger shrieked, shifting into his rabbit and scampering off like a bat out of hell.

I didn't need to ask twice. My town's folk ran like the devil was on their heels. DeeDee sprinted away so quickly, the tape measure floated to the ground five seconds after she was out of sight. I was slightly insulted, but didn't really blame them. My spells occasionally ended with fire works and explosions.

Whatever.

I didn't have time to lambaste them for something I would have done myself. I had business to take care of.

"Goddess on high hear me speak

The town's a mother humpin' mess and needs a magical tweak

Bring Assjacket back to its former battered glory

This place is a fairy tale, not a sad story."

With a wave of my hands, several of the decaying boards splintered with a loud fiery pop and a gust of pink glitter blew through Main Street. Thankfully no three-alarm fire occurred, but the problem remained. The town was still falling apart.

"What the hell?" I shouted, looking around in surprise. "That should have worked."

"Sugar Lips," Fat Bastard said as he waddled over and examined the smoldering boards. Boba Fett and Jango Fett were right on his heels and sniffed at the still burning wood. "You might want to add a few cuss words to that spell. Youse been having better luck with them non-traditional voodoos."

"The cat might be right," Roger concurred, now back in his human form except for his pink nose and whiskers. "Your creative use of the f-bomb seems to add some panache to your spells."

They had a point—a slightly embarrassing one—but a point nonetheless. I was finding my own witchy groove, and alarmingly my spells comprised of potty words had a higher success rate. While I debated which four letter words to include, a sensation similar to déjà vu came over me. And it wasn't a good feeling.

"It's because of the lurking fucking evil," I whispered, positive I was correct.

"What?" Sassy asked as she and Jeeves joined my cats in their investigation of the boards.

For a split second, I completely forgot what I was talking about as I marveled at Jeeves' idea of sportswear. My kangaroo *stepson* had paired lime green jockey breeches with navy Converse hi-tops, white socks, a skin-tight yellow tank and a top hat. It was so wrong it was just… well, it was just *wrong*.

"What was I talking about?" I asked myself and anyone willing to help me out.

"The lurking shit," Fat Bastard reminded me as he too stared at Jeeves in wonderment.

"It's the lurking fucking evil. It has to be," I said, looking away from Jeeves so I could concentrate. I decided I should come up with a spell entirely made up of four letter words. It would be difficult, but doable. I had a vast potty word vocabulary.

"But the lurking fucking evil is gone," Simon, my skunk buddy, reminded me as he covertly moved in front of Jeeves so I could maintain my train of thought. "You destroyed it."

"But we never found the source," Mac said tightly. "I think Zelda's correct. There's no other explanation for something like this."

"We have to find its origin," I said, pacing up and down the crumbling sidewalk trying to figure out what would rhyme nicely with the word jack-hole. I wanted my spells to make a modicum of sense.

I'd become complacent in my happiness. Everything was going so well for the first time in my life, I'd pushed all ugly realities aside. This was my territory and I was supposed to protect it and keep the magical balance. Being hormonal, pregnant, and obsessed with Ho Hos, had overtaken my rational senses. Time to witch up and kick some ass.

"How do we find it?" Wanda asked the logical question that I was currently mulling over myself. "The honey badger Shifters are gone and your mother is imprisoned. The magic-stealing green goop from the syringe was destroyed. As far as we know no one else was working with them."

"It could be Vampyres," Mac said with a shudder of disgust.

"Let's hope not," I replied. "Those wankers are tremendously hard to eliminate. Wanker rhymes with canker."

Everyone was silent for a moment, completely confused by my statement—except for Sassy.

"Shanker, spanker," she added and then expanded the search. "Asshole, poop-bowl, dork-troll, butt-coal."

"Um... you can stop," I told her, beginning to get a bit frightened. However, *poop-bowl* had a nice ring to it.

"Okay, just trying to be helpful."

"Thanks."

"Anytime," she replied.

"Hows bout sphincter-scroll?" Jango Fett added, not wanting to be left out of anything remotely profane.

I had nothing for that one.

Mac cleared his throat and drew the attention of our people away from the certifiable witches and the obscene cats back to the matter at hand.

"We'll patrol in groups of four. The mission is to scour the area," Mac said to the now growing crowd of Shifters.

"What exactly are we looking for?" Bob asked with a nervous twitch.

Mac shrugged his shoulders in frustration. "Not sure," he admitted. "If you notice anything off, or any trace that honey badgers have been in the area, report back immediately."

"What about Vamps?" Jeeves inquired with wide eyes as he tilted his top hat to the left, making him look slightly drunk.

"Any evidence of Vamps and you hightail it back here. I'm the only one who goes after a Vamp," Mac said tersely. "Understood?"

Everyone nodded uneasily and began to whisper amongst themselves.

"We can set up the command station at the diner," Wanda offered.

"No." I shook my head and stopped my incessant pacing. "Too risky in case a human actually does wander in. We can use my new Shifter Wanker office. It's nowhere near the main drag."

"Zelda's right," Mac agreed. "Gather everyone and meet us there in an hour."

The crowd broke apart hastily and I grabbed my father's hand. "What do you think it is?"

"Honestly, I don't know," he said. "However, I'd suggest not using the term sphincter-scroll in a spell. Ever."

"Good point."

"Should we let Baba Yaga know what's happening here?" he asked carefully.

"Nope," I shot back with no hesitation and far more certainty than I felt. "This is my problem, not Baba Yobuttinsky's. I'll solve it."

"As you wish," Fabio said with a smile filled with pride.

It was nine AM. I had three hours before I had to bake with the old witch. However, that was not necessarily a bad thing. An old witch might have some wisdom.

Even a potentially evil witch who lived in a cookie house.

Chapter 9

"We go in rotations," Mac instructed the eight groups of four. "No one works alone. If you find something, shift and alert me."

"You want us to search in human form or animal?" Simon asked.

"Your choice," Mac answered. "Hands might be helpful, but cell phones are spotty in the woods. Shift to your animal if you need to speak with me."

As King, Mac could communicate with his people telepathically. It was all kinds of cool and very useful. Speaking of *not very useful...* my obese cats conjured up a trunk of weapons and dove into it.

Fat Bastard was now armed to the teeth, which was ludicrous since he and my other two cats were furry weapons without any armor needed. Any magic that stuck them flew right back at the attacker.

"We was wonderin' if we was allowed to blow some shit up on this here patrol," Fat Bastard grunted under the weight of his absurd arsenal.

"What do you want to blow up?" I asked, shaking my head and thinking it was not a good idea to send them out into the wilderness armed.

"We was thinking a couple trees and maybe a house or two," Jango informed me while tucking a few cans of spray paint into a bag he then hung around his neck.

"Um, no. And why in the Goddess's name do you need spray paint?" I demanded. I knew exactly what they planned to do. They'd been run out of several towns for profane graffiti.

"We was gonna touch up Main Street, Dollface," Boba Fett explained, looking as innocent as a lying, hairy sack of crap could.

"Hand them over," I said in a take no catshit tone. "If I see one nasty word painted anywhere in Assjacket, all three of you will be getting very familiar with your cat kennels. We clear?"

"As mud," Fat Bastard grumbled. "A guy can't have any fun round here."

"You're a cat. Right now you're a guy cat, but that can be quickly remedied," I informed him. "You want to keep those balls you're so fond of, you will not blow anything up and you will not defile the town."

"Shealmostmadeuseateachothersnutsacksiwouldlisten towhatshesaysshehasaballfetish," Chunk volunteered to a flummoxed crowd.

Sassy and Jeeves patted their new *son* lovingly on the head and looked as confused as the rest of us as to what Chunk had just said.

"If he said anything pertinent, someone needs to translate," Mac said, closing his eyes and breathing deeply.

"Um, not sure if it pertains," Chunk's brother Chip volunteered, smacking on his gum so hard I was sure he'd dislocate his jaw. "But he was basically warning the cats that the Almighty Shifter Wanker Zelda, threatened to make us eat our own nads."

Every single male in attendance doubled over in reflexive terror and groaned.

"For the love of the Goddess," I shouted. "You guys were trying to kill me. I wouldn't have actually made you eat each other's nards."

A few of the men righted themselves, but all of them had not so discretely placed their hands over their jewels.

"So what youse is sayin' is that if we was to paint the town, you was jokin' about removing our giggleberries?" Fat Bastard questioned.

"What the hell did you just call your balls?" I asked, biting down on my lips so I wouldn't laugh. Laughing only encouraged the idiots.

"Not the point, Hot Potato," Fat Bastard pointed out. "But I called 'em giggleberries because when you lick th… "

"Stop," I shrieked, waving my hand and sealing his kitty mouth shut. There we some things in life no one needed to know. "Castration is completely different from ingestion. I was totally serious about your punishment. No graffiti."

"Got it," Jango said with a furry paw shielding his tiny privates. "No graffiti."

"It's ten," Mac said checking his watch, still slightly bent forward. "First four groups go now and second four groups stand watch downtown. Make sure you tag team with the next round when you come back in and then report to me. I want you to stay in groups. No one goes anywhere alone."

Our people dispersed quickly and silently, and went to patrol. The seriousness of the situation hit me. I was about to bring babies into this world. And the world at this very moment wasn't the beautifully magical one I'd always known.

"Fabio, Sassy, and Jeeves... Mac and I will go with you," I said, walking over to them. My gut twisted at the thought of being late for Cookie Witch. She didn't seem to be the most stable of the voodoo crowd. However, if I was late, I was late. I hoped she would understand, but it was what it was. I swore I would come back. I didn't swear I would be on time...

"Zelda, I want you to stay here," Mac said firmly.

"I'm sorry, what?"

"I want you to stay at headquarters," he repeated not making a whole lot of eye contact.

I knew what he was doing, but it wasn't going to fly. My power was stronger than everyone in Assjacket put together. Along with the fact that it was my job to heal and maintain the magical balance, this was my responsibility. I was going.

"Not happening."

Mac ran his hands through his hair, sighed and then took his alpha-hole tone. "You're pregnant. I can't risk anything happening to you or the babies. Period. End of discussion."

"Since when did you become the boss of me?" I demanded as my fingers began to spark and my hair blew dangerously around my head.

"Since right now," Mac replied evenly.

"Interesting," I snapped, stomping over to him and going nose to nose—or rather my nose to his chest. He was much taller than me. Holding my breath so I wouldn't be able to take in how delicious the bossy jackwad smelled, I flicked my fingers and tried to hang his alpha-hole ass in the air to teach him a lesson. However, he just rose an inch or two off the ground. "What the ever lovin' hell?"

Fabio then flicked his own fingers at Mac, but he only rose another few inches. "Our magic has been affected," my dad said, clearly as shocked as I was.

"Wait," Sassy insisted as she too tried to levitate my mate—or so I thought.

As soon as the smoke from her spell cleared, the man of my dreams was clad in a sliver sequined gown and high heels. The look on Mac's face made all of us take a few steps back.

"Oh no, oh no, oh no," Jeeves fretted as he began hopping around in distress.

"Are the three of you done?" Mac asked in a calm voice that belied the very unhappy expression marring his handsome features.

"Almost," I promised quickly as I gripped Sassy by the shoulders. "What exactly did you try to do to him?"

"Well," she said, completely perplexed. "I tried to dress him in a matching outfit to Jeeves. I mean he looks great in the dress and can totally pull off heels, but it's not what I was trying to do."

"I'd wear that dress," Jeeves volunteered, trying to make the fact that his dad was wearing a gown more palatable.

He failed.

"Enough," Mac growled. "Get me down and give me back my clothes."

As Sassy raised her hands to do just that, I tackled her to the ground. "No! Goddess only knows what will happen if you try to reverse the spell. Mac, you're going to have to go up to the house and change. We're a little too dangerous at the moment."

"*At the moment?*" he questioned under his breath, using his own Shifter magic to plant his feet back on solid ground. "No one leaves until I return. Clear?"

It was a little hard to take him seriously in formal pageant wear, but I nodded with what I hoped was a straight face. I knew he was being overbearing because he loved me and the puppies, but I wasn't a helpless little witch. I was an all-powerful... wait. Not right now I wasn't. Shit. I *was* a little dangerous *at the moment.*

As Mac walked away with as much dignity as a man in four-inch heels could muster, I grabbed my father and Sassy. "How in the hell is our magic muted?' I hissed. "The only time I've been powerless was when Babayobuttwad put me in time out."

"It's not just us who have lost power," Fabio said, staring at his hands thoughtfully. "It's everywhere. Can't you feel it?"

"I don't feel any loss of power, just the ability to wield it," I told him as he nodded his head in agreement.

"All I know is that I want to whip up a dress like that for myself," Sassy said, helping very little—as usual.

"Could the lurking fucking evil be doing this?" I asked wondering if I'd even be able to transport to the cookie house for my punishment—or rather the little old witch's punishment. I wasn't exaggerating my lack of cooking skills.

"I don't see how," my dad said. "Evil would suck our magic out. We still have it, although it's seems to be temporarily broken."

"Shit," I muttered as I began to pace and think.

I really didn't want to call on Baba Yaga. This was my territory and I was supposed to take care of it. I shouldn't need my unstable, horribly dressed *mother figure* to have to come and bail me out of a problem. However, this wasn't just a problem, it was a potential clusterfuck.

What to do... what to do...

Dang it, had my lying screwed up the balance? Was that possible? Plenty of witches lied or omitted. My dad was the world champion of evasiveness. However, I was technically still on probation from my stint in the magical pokey. Did I miss some of the fine print? I was well aware that I could only use my magic for the good of others, but fibbing? Damndamndamn.

I could fix this. It wouldn't be pretty, but...

"I ate a house," I confessed.

My dad, Sassy and Jeeves simply stared as if I'd finally snapped.

"Seriously, I did. In my defense, it was made out of cookies, icing, rainbow gum drops and chocolate."

Still radio silence from the trio.

"I have to go and help the old witch fix it. It looks pretty bad. I didn't even realize I'd eaten the door clean off the hinges, but it was chocolate. Of course, the old candy-cane wielding crone could have blasted my ass, but she didn't. My restitution is to go back for a few days and help her re-bake the door, chimney and windowsill. I warned her that I couldn't cook, but she called bullshit on that. She's in for a hell of a nasty surprise."

Silently Fabio approached me and placed his hand on my forehead.

"What are you doing?" I asked, slapping his hand away.

"Checking for a fever."

"I'm a witch. I don't get fevers," I said and then decided while I was on a roll to continue. "I also have a secret stash of Ho Hos. Wait. I don't have that anymore. Mac put them down the disposal except for the one we used for... never mind."

"Should I dive into her head and see if she lost her brain?" Sassy offered, cracking her neck and popping her knuckles in preparation for Goddess only knew what.

"NO," Fabio, Jeeves, and I shouted at the same time.

Sassy had a gift for pulling information out of people's minds. However, she was dangerous under normal circumstances. Being at half magic, who knew what she would do to my gray matter.

"Explain," Fabio said, still staring at me with doubt.

"I already did. But you clearly didn't listen so I'll make it easy for you." Taking in a huge breath, I let it rip. "Since you bribed everyone to eschew carbs for nine months, I had to… "

"Whoa whoa whoa," Sassy shouted. "What does eschew mean? And what the hell language is that?"

"It means to give up," Jeeves told her sweetly as he stared at her with adoration.

"Is it French?" she inquired with narrowed eyes and twitchy fingers.

"No," Fabio said, exasperated.

"Tell your dad about your magical food wand," Sassy tattled since I was confessing my sins.

With an eye roll and a shake of my head, I ignored her jealousy at my fictional wand and focused on my dad. "I had plans to conjure up carbs, but then I had an epiphany while I was flying around the berry patch. I promised Lucky and Charm that I would be a good mom and stop eating shit."

"Two questions," Sassy said, weaseling her way back into the conversation much to Jeeves' great concern for her well being. "Who are Lucky and Charm, and did you really eat shit?"

"If I was at full power right now, you'd be a two foot tall bearded troll," I hissed at her.

"So you did eat shit," she replied, clearly missing my not so subtle hint of threatening to turn her into a hobbit.

"Um... Sassy it's time for our patrol," Jeeves said bouncing up and down in fear for his love's life. His gaze finally met ours for a nanosecond. "We'll be in town if you'd like to join us."

My dad nodded absently, but his attention was still on me. The look of concern on his face made me mad. I was finally telling the truth and he thought I was nuts. I mean I *was* slightly nuts, but I was being honest.

Jeeves picked up a reluctant and babbling Sassy and hopped off into the woods.

"So let me get this straight," Fabio said carefully, staring at me. "You say you found a cookie house in the woods that belongs to an old witch. And you ate the house."

"Only a section of it."

"I see." My dad nodded as if this were a normal everyday conversation.

"I don't think you do. And by the way, the carb-eating fairies you hired were there. Do you have any idea what language they speak? I couldn't make out a word."

"I believe they speak French."

"Seriously?"

"Yes. This old witch, how did you know she was old? It's virtually impossible to judge a witch's age," Fabio said.

I heaved a sigh of relief that he was beginning to believe me. "She had gray hair and walked with a cane—a candy cane."

"Short?"

"Yes."

"Her name?" he asked as he paled a bit.

"She didn't give me a name," I whispered, catching his discomfort. Holy hell on a stick, had I eaten a really evil witch's house?

And then the conversation got better... Mac rejoined us.

Crap.

"I heard everything," Mac said tersely as he walked up dressed in jeans, boots and a flannel shirt.

He looked like he'd just walked off the page of a Ralph Lauren catalogue. It made it a little hard to concentrate, but I ripped my eyes away from him and focused on the matter at hand. I was half tempted to yell Ho Ho because he looked so hot, but my dad being present thankfully put a damper on my sex drive.

"Eavesdropping?" Fabio asked, annoyed.

"Nope," Mac replied with a raised brow. "Werewolf hearing... and you witches talk loud. You ate a house?"

I nodded and hung my head in shame. Playing with the zipper on my jacket, I wanted to cry. How in the hell did I eat a house? It was not sexy to have to explain to your mate that you devoured someone's residence. "Yes. Not the whole thing though."

"Well, there's something at least," Mac said with a grin. "Was it good?"

"Outstanding," I told him with a small smile pulling at my lips.

"It's not funny," Fabio spat. "I only know of one witch who is crazy enough to live in an edible abode and she's supposed to be dead."

We were all silent, lost in our own thoughts of where to take this bizarre conversation. I was definitely sure that Cookie Witch was not a ghost. I'd recently had first hand experience with a ghost when my Aunt Hildy had returned to help save the day. The gingerbread sorceress was one hundred percent *not* dead.

"Cookie Witch isn't dead," I said firmly. "She touched my hair and it didn't freeze me. She can't be dead."

"She touched you?" Fabio hissed.

"Um... yes?" I answered, getting nauseas. Goddess, what had I done? Was I the reason the magic was disappearing because I ate a damn house and let a debatably dead or crazy witch touch my hair. "Did I do this?" I whispered.

"No, you didn't do this," Mac insisted, glancing over at my father. "Did she?"

"We're going with you to the witch," Fabio said, avoiding Mac's question. "Mac you'll go in wolf form and I'll cloak myself."

"You can't," I told him. "Not unless you have some power hidden up your sleeve. Our magic is wonked."

"Damn it, you're right. You're not going."

"Um... yes I am," I shot back. "I ate her chimney and I swore on witch's honor that I would return."

"What time are you meeting her?" Fabio asked. He was clearly very unhappy, but going back on witch's honor was a no-no of unheard of proportions.

"Noon."

Checking his watch, he grimaced. "That gives us enough time to drive out to the berry patch since transporting could land us Goddess knows where."

"All of that's good, but I'm not sure I can find her place on foot," I admitted.

"I can," Mac said with a cocky grin that made me want to jump him and play tonsil hockey. "If you've been there, I can track your scent. I can find you anywhere, baby."

"Goddess, that is so freakin' hot," I said, laying a big wet one on his smiling lips.

"*Hello*. Your father is standing two feet away," Fabio groused. "While I understand that you are a grown, pregnant woman with a mate, I *really* do not want any solid evidence."

"My bad," I apologized, not meaning a word of it.

"You ready?" Fabio asked as he walked over to his SUV.

Mac and I followed behind. He took my hand in his. With a wink and a quick squeeze, he opened the door for me.

"Nope, but when has that ever stopped me?" I said as I climbed in.

"That's my girl," Mac said as he got in the back. "Let's go find the Cookie Witch."

"Do you realize how ridiculous that sounds?" I laughed and let my head fall back on the soft leather seat.

"No more ridiculous than me shifting into a wolf or your father using magic to procure furniture that isn't on the market or... " Mac stated.

"Or me eating a house," I added with a sigh.

"Or you eating a house," he agreed with a chuckle.

Goddess, today couldn't get anymore clusterfucky.

Or could it?

Chapter 10

"You're late," Cookie Witch informed me as I sprinted up her lane, accidentally ripping the chocolate dipped pretzel gate off the hinges in my haste.

Sweating from running through the woods and trying to keep up with Mac's wolf had sucked. Fabio had barely broken a sweat. He'd obnoxiously informed me it was his yoga classes that kept him in top form. Which led me to remind him he'd pilfered my yoga pants and had been dressed like a woman for the past few months of his exercise regimen. Fabdudio just grinned and shrugged leaving my pathetic ass in the dust. I was secretly impressed he didn't give a crap about wearing women's pants.

I knew I was late but my tardiness couldn't be helped. It had been difficult to find the witch's house even with Mac's incredible sense of smell. Normally I didn't sweat—I glistened. Today I was full-out sweating and it wasn't pretty. I was way out of shape or maybe I'd become too dependent on magic to get me where I wanted to go. New item on my list: steal back all my yoga pants from my dad so I could work out like a human. My puppies would be healthier for it.

"Yep," I agreed, handing her the gate with an apologetic smile. "Kind of forgot how to get here."

She examined me critically and then limped to the end of her lane and reattached the gate with a wave of her hand. Cookie Witch's magic did not seem to be affected like mine. Interesting. She glanced off into the woods and huffed and puffed a bit. Damn it, had she spotted Mac and my dad? I couldn't spot either one of them and I knew where they were. Fabio had reluctantly agreed to stay hidden in the woods. Cookie Witch would be aware of his presence if he were too close since cloaking was impossible at half power. Crapballs, I needed a distraction.

"I'm ready to bake or possibly burn your house down with my cooking prowess," I announced. I put my hands on her shoulders and gently turned her away from the woods while I escorted her little body back toward the house. Her limp was pronounced and I wondered why she wasn't using her cane. Cookie Witch was solid—definitely not a ghost. My hands would have gone right through her and I would have been frozen like a block of ice.

Motherhumper, I hadn't thought of that little possibility when I touched her due to my fear of her seeing Mac and my dad. Needing to stay focused and on top of the fact that I was providing room and board for two little beings in my belly, I promised myself to proceed with more caution.

"Not so fast, Zeldoumannawanna," she said, twisting out from beneath my hands but grabbing my arm for purchase. "Why are you late?"

"Because… " I hedged trying to come up with something that had a modicum of truth to it. It was still a possibility that my lying had something to do with the absence of magic in the area. "Because there were a few issues in Assjacket I had to deal with."

"Assjacket?" she inquired with squinted eyes and pursed lips.

"Yep, that's my town," I told her with confidence. I knew damn well it wasn't the real name of my town, but it was the Goddess's honest truth that I called my new home Assjacket. The less she knew about where I lived the better.

"Can't say I know Assjacket," she said with a brow arched so high I would swear it touched her hairline. "What exactly do you do in Assjacket, Zeldoumannawanna?"

Deciding to play her game I raised my own brows. Of course my arch was not nearly as impressive as hers, but still, I was no slouch. "I live there. What do you do in the berry patch?"

Her chuckle made her seem like a sweet little witch, but I wasn't falling for anything today. "I live here," she replied with an answer equally as cryptic as my own.

"Mmmkay," I said with an eye roll. "Now that we've bonded, why don't we get down to business? And not to be forward or anything, but if you want me to, I could possibly help you out with that limp you've got going there."

I waited for her to zap me or berate me.

She didn't disappoint.

Her eyes narrowed and she hissed with displeasure. "You think you're all high and mighty because you're a healer?" she demanded as I backed away from her sparking fingers. "I don't need your magic or your pity, girlie. I'm fine just the way I am and if don't like it you can take your judgmental self home right now."

"Actually, I can't," I told her. "I gave you my word on witch's honor that I'd return and re-bake your house. Sorry for trying to help. Won't make that mistake again."

"Damn right you won't, girlie," she muttered and walked into her house leaving me on the stoop.

"Your manners are lovely. I didn't want to heal you anyway. It probably would have hurt more than healing a Shifter with a cracked skull, you nasty old cow with a cookie house. Who in the hell did I screw over that I get to deal with all the bat shit crazy ones?" I muttered under my breath.

"Heard that," she yelled from inside.

"Shitballs, didn't mean any of it," I yelled back and then blanched. No. More. Lying. "Great Goddess in a see through Speedo, I meant every word of it. And I'm sorry... that you heard it... not that I said it."

Not lying was going to get me killed. Soon.

"Get in the house before the Goddess zaps your sorry ass for dressing her in a Speedo, Zeldoumannawanna," Cookie Witch grumbled.

"Good thinking. Oh and my name isn't really Zeldoumannawanna. It's Zelda."

Coming clean was good, but I had ulterior motives. I wanted her name. Fabio told me the he suspected she was actually a witch named Marge. Once I'd stopped snorting at the ridiculous name, he'd cautioned me that Marge was out of her mind and had been banished hundreds of years ago for all sorts of crimes. Or maybe she'd insulted one of the Baba Yaga's outfits. He couldn't remember...

That didn't exactly help in gauging how dangerous she might be, but it was all I had to go on. Since no one had heard anything about Marge for centuries, she was presumed dead.

"I knew that," she replied.

"Do you have a name?" I inquired politely as I covertly pinched off a little of the door frame and popped it in my mouth.

"I do."

"And?"

"And I'll tell you in good time," she snapped, ending the getting to know you part of our conversation.

The inside of Cookie Witch's house was equally as magical as the outside. Thankfully it wasn't edible or I would have been in enormous trouble. The furniture was squishy and cozy—overstuffed chairs in brightly colored stripes and florals. Puffy ottomans with painted ceramic legs were dotted all over. The hardwood floors were painted in a faded cornflower blue and white checkerboard pattern and the stone fireplace had shimmering glass beads embedded in the rock.

"Oh my Goddess," I gushed, fingering a lamp trimmed in sparkling feathers and beads. "This is beautiful. Where did you get this stuff?"

"Made it," she grumbled, yanking pots and pans out of the cherry wood cabinets.

"With magic?" I asked, attempting to help only to be swatted away.

"With my hands," she shot back with that eyebrow cocked up again. "Already told you once girlie that magic doesn't solve everything. In the end, very little can be solved with magic."

I shrugged noncommittally and wandered around her small house looking for clues. Of what, I had no idea, but I was gonna use my time wisely. Maybe the lurking fucking evil was here. Or maybe Cookie Witch had plans to bake me into a big cookie to replace her door I ate.

Goddess—that was certainly a heinous thought. She was definitely mean and cranky enough to do it. "Are you going to bake me into a cookie door?" I asked, figuring we should get everything out on the table.

"No, girlie. Not today. I only bake people into doors on Thursdays."

Well, that was certainly a relief—kind of. She had a gleam in her eye. Was that humor or batshit craziness? I made a mental note never to come here on a Thursday on the off chance she was serious.

"Do you hate being a witch?" I asked carefully. I didn't want to piss her off more and make her rethink her Thursday rule, but since I was here. I might as well make the most of it. She was a mystery and something was compelling me to know more. She was a powerful witch who clearly had issues with magic. That was pretty messed up.

"Well, do you?" I asked again, when she did answer.

"Nope." Cookie Witch sighed and rested her gnarled hands on the counter. "Some things are not always as they seem. Take the nuclear bomb for example."

I nodded even though I was in utter confusion. What did the nuclear bomb have to do with being a witch? I casually took a seat on the far side of the charming kitchen table with adorable woven place mats. It was the seat closest to the door just in case I had to make a run for it.

"Not really following," I said, pretty sure she had plans to cook me up and turn me into a door. She was nuts.

"Nuclear energy was made with the noblest of intentions and then BOOM!" she shouted as I scrambled for the exit.

"Maybe I should come back another time," I offered. "You seem to be a little, um… distracted right now."

"Not distracted at all," she replied as she waved her hands and produced her candy walking-cane. "Did you understand what I said?"

"Um… was I supposed to?"

She sighed and ushered me back to the table. I sat on the edge of my chair on the very likely possibility she lost her marbles again and I had to sprint the hell out.

91

"My point is that magic is like nuclear energy. The Goddess gave us this gift to heal and take care of our earth, but many have misused it—like nuclear energy. The intention was good but the reality was truly horrifying."

"Not everyone misuses magic," I countered.

"You did," she replied.

She had me there, but… "Yes, I did. However, I never harmed anyone. I was selfish and stupid but I've changed—mostly. Maybe I'm still a little selfish and stupid, but I really do mean well."

She nodded and offered me a bowl of chocolate covered peanuts. It wasn't on my new diet, but I wanted to be polite so I ate some—and then some more—and then some more.

"You're transgressions are not actually what I'm referring to even though I do sense some darkness in you. The only one you ever really harmed was yourself," she said, examining the empty bowl with amusement. "I'm speaking of those that use magic expressly for evil. They can't be controlled."

"I disagree," I said, kind of insulted but more surprised that she knew I possessed dark magic as well as light. In removing my mother's magic, I'd taken it into myself. Not my choice. I did what I had to do, but of course now I was stuck with some yicky power as well as the good I was born with and what my Aunt Hildy had given me. Basically, I was a freak of voodoo nature.

She stood up and limped over to the sink with the empty bowl. "That's your prerogative, girlie," she replied with a shrug.

"My name is Zelda," I reminded her.

"Yep," she agreed.

This was going swimmingly.

"Can I guess your name?" I asked casually, wanting to change the subject to something that was more important than comparing magic to a bomb that killed people.

"Good luck with that," she challenged, putting two big bags of white powdery stuff and a bottle of brown liquid on the table.

"What the hell is that?" I asked, eyeing the bags warily.

She blew out a long slow breath that smelled like brownies and rolled her eyes. "You weren't lying when you said you couldn't cook, were you?"

"Nope," I confirmed with pride, delighted not to lie. "I burn water. For real."

With a put upon sigh, she held up a stick of yellow stuff. I totally knew what it was.

"Butter," I shouted, relieved I knew something.

The Cookie Witch jumped about a foot off the ground inadvertently blowing up an ottoman and then placed her hand over her rapidly beating heart.

"Sorry," I muttered, helping her to a chair. "That's butter. I'd be happy to eat that if we don't need it to bake."

"You'd eat a stick of butter?" she asked, making a horrified face. "What is wrong with you, girl?"

"Um... nothing?"

We sat in silence and stared at each other. Her eyes, under bushy and constantly arched brows, were a lovely shade of light purple. My guess was that she'd been a beauty in her day—whenever the hell that had been. I was beginning to think this was a waste of my time considering what was going on in Assjacket. However, I had to pay the piper—or the witch—for eating her place of residence.

"Can we get the show on the road?" I asked, trying to be tactful.

"Do you know what that is?" she asked pointing to the bags of powder on the table.

"Baking stuff?"

"Lost cause," she muttered and began slamming the *baking stuff* back into the cabinets.

Crappitycrap.

"Look Cookie Witch, I'm sorry," I said, backing up to the door. "I don't know how to make food unless it comes in a microwave container. I never had a mother who baked or even cooked that much. Before I spent an inordinate time in the pokey for conjuring up Jimmy Choo's and expensive vacations, I used to eat out a lot or just wiggle my fingers and magic up a cheeseburger and French fries. I'm good at a lot of shit, but cooking is not one of them."

"You done?"

"Nope. I'm on a roll. Now I'm only allowed to use my magic for the good of others because Baba Yostankyass put me on probation after my release from the Big House. I secretly like the stipulation, but it's screwed with my street cred as an uncaring loner. However, I know I *never* used my magic like a nuclear bomb," I told her, hoping to avoid her blowing anything else up—including me.

"Done yet?"

"Close," I assured her. "You're kind of the least of my problems right now. Assjacket in is crisis. I have three fat ass familiars on the loose who enjoy defacing property with profane graffiti. My dad has bribed everyone in town to give up carbs for nine months and I'm pregnant with puppies for the love of the Goddess. Eating your house was a necessary mistake."

Groaning, I smacked my forehead. "No! It wasn't a mistake. I've gone off lying just in case I'm the cause of the clusterfuck. I ate your house on purpose. But I would like to point out you're a little insane to have an edible house and not expect pregnant people to eat it."

When she looked confused, I plunged on. "I mean, you're kind of living the stereotype of an evil child-eating witch living in a gingerbread house. However, I'm not one to judge considering I recently starred in a musical version of *Mommie Dearest*. So as you can see, I have a few problems to deal with back at home, so if you're gonna smite my ass go ahead and get it over with."

She just stared open-mouthed at me as I turned around and prepared to get my butt fried.

"And even though you're rude, cranky and basically socially unacceptable, I'm still willing to heal your limp."

She said nothing—just stared at me strangely.

"Now I'm done," I added over my shoulder.

"*Cookie Witch?*" she inquired, trying to hide her smirk.

"Um… yes," I admitted. "Didn't know what else to call you."

"Baba Yostankyass?"

"That came out a little wrong," I said and then slapped my forehead again. That was a bald face lie. "No it didn't," I confessed quickly. "I meant it. That's just one of the names I call her."

"She *is* a royal back-stabbing skank-hole," Cookie Witch muttered as she continued to put the pans and bowls away.

Wait one small minute.

My stomach clenched in fury and my hair began to blow around my head. My fingers sparked and my magic roared inside my body. Cookie Witch had just broken a sacred rule. Baba Yopaininmybutt was mine to insult. She was family to me in a weird unrelated, semi-dysfunctional way. I could say whatever I wanted about her because I secretly loved her. Of course, I would never admit it in public, but I did love her. And I was pretty sure she loved me—well, at the very least she liked me a lot. This little old biddy could not say bad things about the fashion impaired, whack job leader of all witches.

"Take it back," I hissed as I realized I was at full power again. "You will not disrespect Baba Yomamma in my presence. *Shit*," I shouted and banged the back of my head against the wall. "I meant Baba Yaga. *Baba. Yaga.* NO, I meant Baba Yomamma," I admitted in my outdoor voice. Damn it to hell it was hard not to lie. "However, I love her and I can say that. You can't. And if you tell anyone I love her, I will deny it and eat your entire house in one sitting."

"Tamp it down, girlie," she said not even turning around. "Carol knows I think she's a gaping wad of sewage. She thinks I'm one as well. You? You simply surprise me."

Now I was seriously confused. My power swirled but I kept it in check while I got to the bottom of this mystery.

"Because I could eat your entire house?"

"Nope."

She was clearly not going to explain herself. Fine. I'd pry out what I could and get the hell out.

"You know Carol?" I asked warily as I reined in my power. My gut said Cookie Witch wasn't evil—just insane—but my gut could be wildly wrong. And why did I surprise her?

Cookie Witch refused to answer me. She wiped down her counters and removed her apron.

"We're done for the afternoon," she informed me. "You will come back tomorrow at the same time. You can tell your wolf that I can see through the trees and boulders, so hiding is useless. And tell your father, *Marge* says hello."

Before I could scream—before I could run—before I could raise my hands to zap her evil Cookie Witch ass, I was whipped up in another brownie scented tornado and whisked out of her house. Instead of fighting it, I relaxed and prayed to the Goddess she was retuning me to the car.

She was.

I landed in a heap near the SUV. My shocked father landed about three feet from me and Mac showed up in his own tornado about three seconds later. I ran my hands over my body and realized I was totally unharmed. Lucky and Charm sent a ticklish wave through my body and I almost cried in relief.

"What the hell just happened?" Mac demanded, sprinting over to me and checking me out from head to toe for injuries. He was back in his human form and was wildly confused and concerned. "I was watching you and then I was flying through the air in a bakery scented wall of wind."

"I think we might have a problem," I said, taking Mac's offered hand and standing up.

"You think Cookie Witch is the lurking fucking evil?" Mac asked, continuing to check me out for anything out of the ordinary.

"No, I don't think she's evil. She's crazy and weird and old, but... "

"But what?" Fabio demanded impatiently. "What did she say?"

My father was a wreck. His hair was standing straight up on his head and he was pale. He took his daddy role seriously and I knew it had made him insane to let me go alone to the Cookie Witch. Before I was pregnant, I'd simply laughed off all of his ridiculous concerns—but not anymore.

"She told me to tell you hello from Marge."

"Oh shit," he shouted and grabbed onto the car for support.

"And then some... " I finished for him.

Chapter 11

"I don't want to, but I should summon Baba Yaga," I said, pacing my kitchen in agitation. "Marge knows Carol and Carol knows why Marge was banished... Maybe. However, if Baba Yoyohead gets involved, this clusterhump could morph into a clusterfuck."

The morning had dawned bright, sunny and cold. There was a wonderful crispness in the air, but there was far less magic present—not good. My three fat cats, Mac, and my father sat at our kitchen table and listened to me ramble. No one on patrol had found any evidence of honey badgers, vamps, or lurking fucking evil. However, they all found that the magic in the area was waning dangerously.

The problem had to stem from Marge the Cookie Witch. I couldn't quite figure out how, but it had to. At this point I prayed to the Goddess it did, otherwise we had no leads whatsoever.

"Could she be glamouring herself to appear old?" I asked my dad.

"Could be," he surmised with a nod, but an expression of doubt. "But the Marge I remember was seriously vain and wouldn't be caught dead with a hair out of place."

"Don't make no sense," Fat Bastard said, coming up for air while taking a respite from grooming his jewels. "You says you had your magic in the hairy snatch?"

"Berry patch," I corrected him with a wince of disgust.

"S'what I said," he went on. "The Nookie Snitch had her power too?"

"Cookie Witch," I corrected him again.

"Yeah, whatever," he dismissed me with an eye roll and crotch grab. "So as I was sayin' the Rookie Bitch... she has her magic?"

"Yes," I replied, trying my damnedest to overlook his hearing problem without throwing something at him or knocking his furry noggin into the wall.

"I believe the Bastard might need a hearing aid," Fabio said, narrowing his eyes at my cat.

"Nah," Fat Bastard explained with an evil little kitty laugh. "I just like to fark with Zelda. Good times."

"Lovely," I muttered as I picked up an entire head of lettuce and bit into it like it was an apple. Not the tastiest breakfast, but it was the closest thing edible.

"Point being," Fat Bastard went on. "Magic still works there, but no wheres else."

"What do you mean no where else?" I demanded through a mouth full of salad greens.

"Word's out that magic around the world has gone on the fritz," Fabio said. "It's not just here in Assjacket."

"Does it bother anyone that the name of the town isn't actually Assjacket?" Mac asked, pressing his fingers to the bridge of his nose.

"No," we all replied at once.

"Alrighty then," he said and handed me a bowl of fruit to go with the tasteless leaves in my mouth.

"So if Cookie Witch's magic works, she must be doing something to keep the area up," I said, thinking out loud. "Maybe she's pulling on all the magic around the world so she has the best berries ever."

"Lame," Jango Fett grunted not even glancing up from his nut cleansing.

"I know," I snapped. "I'm just yanking stuff out of my ass at this point."

"For real?" Jango asked with great interest as he took a brief ball licking break to see if I was being literal.

"Um… no, you dork. I'm just hoping if I talk enough something will make sense."

"Now there's a scary plan," Fat Bastard mumbled.

"Tell me again what she said," Fabio suggested, giving the Bastard a look that made him shut his cakehole.

"Well, she compared magic to nuclear energy," I told him as I slathered an apple in peanut butter and hot sauce. "Said witches use it for evil and they can't be stopped. She also got grossed out that I offered to eat a stick of butter."

My men were smart. No one made a comment on my desire to eat lard. And then much to my shock and dismay, the peaceful atmosphere in my kitchen changed on a dime.

"Incoming," Boba Fett shrieked as he dove for cover.

"Shit," I hissed as I too took cover. Baba Yaga's entrances were infamous and occasionally dangerous.

The room filled with glowing purple smoke and sparkling blue bubbles. A mirror ball set to vomit inducing speed attached itself to the ceiling and the soundtrack from *Desperately Seeking Susan* bounced off the walls of the vast kitchen. Since Madonna was Baba Yostuckintheeighties' idol, the music didn't surprise me. The fact that Baba Yaga showed up without her posse of bobbleheaded warlocks did. She rarely travelled without the snarky little fuckers.

101

"Hello darling," Baba Yaga trilled, giving me an air kiss before laying a lip lock on my dad that belonged behind closed doors.

"Um… gross," I said, covering my eyes and groaning. "To what do we owe this alarming visit and yucky display of affection? And where are your stinky minions?"

"Interesting you should ask," she replied as she wiped the smeared hot pink lipstick from my father's grinning mouth. "Seems there's a magical shortage. That's why my cranky posse isn't here. Too risky that one of them could land Goddess only knows where."

"Would that be such a bad thing?" I asked, biting back my smile. They were annoying, judgmental and rude. I didn't know anyone who liked them—except for Baba Yaga.

"Touché," she replied easily as she took in my peanut butter-hot sauce-fruit snack with a moue of disgust. "They come in handy. You'll see one day when you take over for me and inherit them."

"Oh, *hell* to the no!" I shouted and let my head fall to the table with a thud. "I really, really think you should find another successor. I am not cut out to be a Baba Yaga. *Ever.* I'm still getting a grip on healing furry freaks as the Shifter Wanker. You really don't want me leading our kind."

"Too bad, so sad," Baba sang as she gyrated to *Get Into the Groove.*

Her dancing was appalling, but her outfit was positively gag worthy—aqua green parachute pants paired with a *Flashdance*-ripped pink sweat shirt and Nike Air Pythons on her feet. Her bangs were teased and sprayed within an inch of their unfortunate life and she had at least a hundred black rubber bracelets on each arm. Imagining her closet made me shudder in terror. It would be like getting trapped in the bowels of Hell.

"Marge called you a name—an ugly one," I told her.

Her dancing halted, the music died and Baba Yoscary Witch replaced the happy, horribly clad woman who was present only seconds ago. With her eyes narrowed to slits, she approached me slowly. I stood my ground. She wasn't pissed at me... I hoped.

"Did you say *Marge?*"

I nodded carefully. Clearly this wasn't welcome news.

"Marge is dead," she growled.

"Um... I don't think so," I whispered.

"I'm quite certain she's residing in Hell," Baba insisted at full volume as little sparks of pissed off magic swirled around her. "I would have run into her in the last several hundred years if the old hag was still breathing."

While Baba's voice was strong, the uncertainty in her eyes was odd and slightly unnerving. What in the Goddesses name was really going on here?

"She's not dead and she's not a ghost. Cookie Witch is old, gray and she limps, but she's very much alive. And she lives in a cookie house—hence the name," I said, watching closely for Baba's reaction.

"She lives in a *cookie house?*" Baba asked with what I could have sworn was a small smile pulling at her lips, but it disappeared quickly.

"Yes and I ate part of it," I admitted.

"You *ate* Marge's house and lived to tell?" she demanded, gaping at me.

"Do I look dead to you?" I snapped, clearly coming unhinged since I couldn't stop back- talking the leader of all witches. I didn't care. I was pregnant and there was a problem. Bringing puppies into the world had either made me more fearless or more unbalanced—I preferred to think fearless. Fixing the problem so the world would be right for my children was my main focus. I needed to solve it more than I needed to kiss Baba Yobossy's ass. Plus I was getting tired of being judged for eating a house. "And I didn't eat the whole thing—only the door, window sill, and a portion of the chimney. However, I did threaten to eat the whole thing if she called you anymore names."

"I don't believe it's her," Baba Yaga said. "However, I find your defense of me lovely and somewhat appalling. You'd actually eat an entire house?"

"I'd try."

"I'd lay money she could eat two houses," Jango Fett chimed in. "With them buns in the oven, she's a fracking eatin' machine."

"I'd bet on three—depending on the size. Was the house one story or two?" Fat Bastard inquired.

"One," Fabio volunteered, sitting on his hands and looking slightly constipated.

I could tell my gambling addicted father was trying his very best not to get in on the wager. It was a good move since I was ready to try out my iffy magic on the next person who felt the need to expound on my house eating.

"Enough," Mac growled. "One more word about Zelda's voracious and alarming appetite and the offender will lose an appendage."

"Thank you, babe... I think," I told Mac.

"No decapitation inside the house," Baba Yaga warned. "I'm not sure Zelda can heal anyone at the moment with the magic being so low. None of you people with a penis can understand what it's like to be pregnant. Only women can. So any more cracks and I'll adjust your plumbing so you'll understand what a trial being female can be."

"You're a mother?" I asked surprised. Certainly I would have known if Baba Yaga had children. Wouldn't I?

"No, darling, not yet. But your father and I are working on it."

"Oh my Goddess," I shrieked. "You've just added several more decades of therapy to my schedule. Roger's going to shit."

"I'd love to have a little me," she went on completely oblivious to the wide-eyed shock of everyone in the room—including my dad. "I'd whip up the cutest little matching outfit for us!"

"Um... while that's somewhat nightmare inducing, maybe we should deal with the Marge issue first," I offered trying to block out the visual of a baby dressed like Madonna, circa 1985.

"I still don't think it's the same Marge," Baba said, thankfully moving on from any conversation that conjured up visuals in my brain of her and my dad even remotely naked.

She sat down at the table and ran her hands through her hair. However, her fingers got stuck in her rock hard bangs and she had to use a little magic to remove them without tearing her bangs clean off of her head. The most amazing thing was that she was still breathtakingly gorgeous with her awful hair and heinous get up.

"I don't know if it's the same Marge you and Fabdudio are referring to and I don't care. I believe she's the key to the lack of magic and I'm going back. Period."

"What exactly did she call me?"

"A royal back-stabbing skank hole."

Baba's laugh was not a happy one. Mac's and my kitchen table now sported an enormous charred hole right smack in the center due to Baba's fury. She jumped to her feet, pulled me out of my chair, and yanked the queso-covered banana I'd just created out of my hands.

"It's definitely Marge. No one is stupid enough to insult me like that except that obnoxious old ass monkey. You're going to pay her a visit and I'm coming along for the ride," she hissed as a rainbow of sparkles hovered menacingly around her body. "That nut job has some explaining to do."

Baba stomped out of the house, swearing and mumbling. The cats were wildly amused and excited by the turn of events, but not Mac and my dad.

"This is a very bad idea," Mac said, grabbing a coat for me and helping me into it. "I'm coming too and I'm not hiding in the woods this time."

I nodded silently and absently rubbed my stomach. I didn't know if I was comforting my unborn children or myself. The day had started off odd and now was quickly careening into something dangerous and potentially deadly.

"I'm going as well," Fabio said. "You and Carol are powerful, but if it's really Marge... she's industrial strength."

"Shit," I muttered, quickly making my way to the door.

"Youse said it, Sweet Cheeks," Fat Bastard grunted, with a grim expression—more serious than I'd ever seen my obese cat look.

"Are we ready?" I asked my nearest and dearest.

"Do we have a choice?" Fabio replied with a worried shrug.

"Nope. Let's do it."

And we did.

Chapter 12

"Explain to me again why we're driving?" Baba complained as she channel-surfed the radio for an eighties station.

"Because there are four people and three fat cats on this field trip to hell. No one has enough magic at the moment to poof us to the berry patch without the risk of someone ending up wedged in a black hole somewhere," I explained for the third time in ten minutes. She was worse than a child and if she asked "Are we there yet?" one more time, I was going to put her out of the car.

"Right," Baba said. "This is just so mundane. I'm not used to this human mode of travel—very time consuming."

"Well, if we don't figure out what the magic drain is, we'll all be traveling like this from now on," I said.

That certainly shut everyone up for a blessedly quiet three minutes.

Mac held me close and my cats were curled up all around me—thankfully on a grooming break. Fabio drove and Baba bitched—one big extremely weird and debatably happy family.

"Are we there yet?" Baba Yaga asked, bouncing up and down to an A Flock of Seagulls song that sadly was going to be stuck in my brain for weeks.

"Almost, my love," Fabio answered. "The berry patch is a wrinkle in time—a bit difficult to find."

"I'm sorry, did you say *wrinkle*?" Baba shouted, turning off the radio and shuddering.

"The Shifters said it was a wrinkle," I told her. "I think Cookie Witch has just spelled it or placed heavy wards."

"Can this place be found on a map?" Baba demanded in her scary all business tone.

"Nope," Mac replied. "It doesn't exist."

"How long has it been there?" she further questioned.

"I've known of it for about fifty years," Mac said. "Don't know how long it existed before that."

"Is it bad if it's a wrinkle in time?" I asked, sitting up and leaning over the seat.

"No, not necessarily," Baba said thoughtfully. "It just means it's definitely Marge. It's one of her gifts. She's a Creator Witch—like me."

"What in the Goddess's name is happening?" Fabio hissed as the car lost power and rolled to a slow stop at the outer edge of the berry patch. "Car's dead."

He turned the ignition several times with no luck. Everyone hopped out and stood at the end of the path that led to the magical area. Power vibrated off the perimeter of the patch and the beauty was astounding.

"Interesting," Baba purred, reapplying her lipstick and peeking under the hood of the car.

"Do you even know what you're looking for?" I asked her trying not to laugh.

"No clue darling, but it seems like the reasonable thing to do," she replied with a wink.

"It's fine," Mac said as he examined the engine. "No fault with the car. It's the magic."

"Awesome. We're going in on foot," I griped.

And so we did—kind of.

"Stand the fark back," Jango Fett grunted as he and my other two cats prepared themselves to be the first in.

Of course *preparing* meant grabbing their little kitty nuts and doing something akin to a profane version of the Haka. It was every kind of wrong. My dad shook his head and checked his watch while Mac just groaned and stared up at the sky.

"Is this really *necessary*?" Baba Yaga asked, wincing as my feline dumbasses all racked each other to determine who was the manliest—or stupidest.

"No, but it's kind of alarmingly funny," I replied. "Since I've been pregnant, they feel the need to protect me more."

"And this is how they do it?" she inquired with arched brows and an appalled expression on her lovely face.

"Um… yes. Just be thankful it's only an audience of four. At the town potluck two weeks ago, this went on for an hour."

"Lovely," Baba Yaga replied dryly.

"Follow us," Jango instructed as he and his two idiot counterparts sprinted toward the entrance of the berry patch.

However, they didn't get far.

"What in the farking voodoo loving hell was that?" Fat Bastard shouted as he flew back through the air and landed in a pissed off heap at my feet.

"Oh my Goddess," I said as I picked up my furry tub of lard and checked him for injury.

"We gots a problem here," Fat Bastard announced after trying three more times to enter the patch and getting violently thrown back with each attempt. "Looks like the Hookie Glitch don't want no visitors today."

"It's warded," Fabio said, making symbols in the air to test the strength of the spell." And it's a doozy."

"I can't walk through it," Mac said in frustration as he pressed his hands against the ward.

"I could pee on it," Fat Bastard offered.

"Would that help?" I asked, confused.

"Nope, but it would be satisfying," he explained.

"Oh for the Goddess's sake," Baba Yaga groused. "Out of my way."

She marched forward and walked right through the ward that held Mac, Dad, and the cats out.

"Come along Zelda," she insisted.

"Wait," Mac shouted as I approached the invisible wall that Baba Yonotscaredofanything had just traipsed through.

Mac took me by the shoulders and kissed me so hard that my head spun and my knees wobbled. My big strong wolf seemed unsure and pissed.

"I want to tell you not to go in there," he ground out, holding on to his cool by a thread. His beautiful eyes searched mine and I felt his fear. "My instincts are to pick you up, throw you in the car and leave... but I won't. It's killing me, but I won't."

"Car don't work anyways," Fat Bastard offered, waddling over and wedging his round body in between us. "If youse are gonna do it, I'd suggest shifting to your wolf and we's could strap her to your back. And if she don't like it, we's can sit on her."

"I'm in," Jango Fett said.

111

"I'd be happy to ride Zelda," Boba Fett added.

"Shut it," Mac growled at the ever unhelpful cats, and then turned his focus back to me. "I will never stop you from what you have to do, but it doesn't mean I'll like it." He approached the edge of the ward and pointed at Baba Yaga. "How do you know Zelda can enter? Can you guarantee her safety and that of our children?" he demanded tightly.

"I can," she snapped. "Put your finger down, wolf. Remember to whom you're growling at. Zelda is the future Baba Yaga. No ward can hold us—it's a perk. And yes, the babies will be fine."

"You know this how?" Mac shot back, uncaring that little sparks of displeasure were wafting around Baba.

She rolled her eyes and stomped around for a bit. Clearly Carol wasn't used to being questioned or distrusted. "Only because you love her to the exclusion of common sense will I overlook your insolent behavior. Never would I lead one of mine into danger knowingly."

"And if you didn't *know*?" he prodded.

"Then I wouldn't do it," she hissed. "Not that I *have* to explain myself... but you have my word *and* the Goddess's that Zelda and your unborn children can pass the ward unharmed. Happy now?" she shouted.

"No, but I'm relieved," he replied coolly.

"Carol's correct," I whispered to the man who had my back in a way I'd never experienced. His bravery—or foolishness—at going head to head with the most powerful witch in the world humbled me and made me love him more than I did even moments ago. "I feel no malice from the ward. And I also think Cookie Witch is very aware of what she's doing. She might not know about Carol's surprise visit, but for some reason she didn't want you or Fabio back in."

"If she means no harm, then why keep us out?" Fabio questioned as he too looked uncomfortable with the turn of events.

"Not sure," I admitted. "But I'm at full magic in the berry patch. Marge knows this and she knows I possess dark magic. I'll zap her like a bug if I have to."

"Promise?" Fabio asked taking my face in his hands.

"Witch's honor."

"I still don't like this, but I'm deferring to you," Mac said with an expression on his face that looked like he'd swallowed a lemon.

"That was really hard for you, wasn't it?" I asked as I grinned up at him.

"Yes. Yes it was," he confessed with a lopsided smile. "However, I'm gathering the troops and we're going to surround the perimeter of the patch. Can you break the ward if you have to?" he asked of Baba.

"Possibly," she said. "I would only do it in a dire emergency. We don't know exactly why Marge set it. We're simply surmising. There could be something far worse than some Shifters that the crazy old ass monkey is trying to keep out."

"She's right," I said, considering the possibility. It was out there, but it was still within the realm. "Maybe it's for your protection."

"Come along, Zelda. We're burning daylight and I'm getting bored," Baba Yaga insisted.

"You'll be careful and you *will* come back to me," Mac informed me in his alpha dude voice. It was all kinds of hot and sexy.

"Yeah, you gotsta come back. It's Goodie Table Night at the diner," Fat Bastard added.

For a second I got really excited and then deflated like a popped balloon. "What good is Goodie Table Night without carbs? As the Goddess is my witness, I will never eat a tofu meatball again. I will go hungry instead. Those things taste like butt."

"Youse know what butt tastes like?" Jango Fett asked, surprised and impressed.

"No," I snapped. "It smells like butt so I'm assuming it has to taste like butt."

"Never assume," Baba Yaga chimed in with a laugh. "It makes an ass out of you."

"You forgot the second part of the adage," I grumbled.

"Nope, I'm not an ass," she stated with glee.

"Whatever. Goodie Table Night has tragically lost its appeal. I'll simply starve—to death—and waste away to nothing. I will live through this heinous ban on carbs and when it's over—if I make it through it, I will never be hungry again—or something like that."

"Fine, *Scarlett O'Hara*," Fabio shouted, throwing his hands in the air and giving up. "I will lift the ban on carbs as long as you come back safe and sound and promise to eat fruits and vegetables along with Ho Hos."

"Um… aren't you going to owe a lot of money to the townsfolk if you change the rules?" I asked with a giggle.

"Money is absolutely immaterial where you are concerned," Fabio huffed, insulted. "I'd trade my life for yours."

"Me too," Fat Bastard grunted.

"Me three," Jango chimed in.

"Four," Boba Fett added with a pelvic thrust.

"And me five," Mac whispered in my ear as he walked me to the edge of the ward. "You are loved, my mate. Be safe and be quick. I'm jonesing for a Ho Ho."

I was torn between laughing and crying. A little happy zing shot through my tummy. Lucky and Charm loved me too. I had no clue what I had done right to deserve this kind of life, but I was going to hold onto it with both of my hands and my whole heart. The magical world around us was crumbling and I knew deep within me that I could fix it—at least I hoped I could. I owed it to my family, my people and my puppies. I had a mission I was going to accomplish.

I just prayed it wouldn't be impossible...

Chapter 13

"Son of a bitch," I muttered, glancing around in confusion after we'd hoofed it for about fifteen minutes and ended up back where we'd started. "Um… I can't remember how to get there."

"No duh," Baba griped, snapping her fingers and creating a small pool of sparkling blue water. Yanking off her hot pink faux fur jacket that could have passed for a bad 70's shag throw rug, she got down on her knees and checked out her reflection.

"Wouldn't it have been easier to conjure up a mirror?"

"You can't scry with a mirror," she shot back.

I shrugged in embarrassment and shut my mouth. She was a bazillion years old and I was thirty. I might be a smart-ass, but I wasn't stupid. Slipping off my coat, I sat down next to her and peeked into the water. Baba chanted in a hypnotically beautiful rhythm. The air was warm and balmy. The weather and the berry patch itself were bizarre. Strangely, I felt comfortable and safe here.

"It's not working," Baba snapped in frustration. She waved her hands displaying her perfectly manicured nails and made the pool disappear back into the lush green earth. "The old biddy's hidden herself well."

"Why?"

"Well, darling that's what we're here to find out, isn't it?" she replied slapping her hands on her hips and staring pointedly at me. "Can you poof us there?"

"I don't think so. Even though I've been, I can't really remember where it is."

"Hmmm... doesn't surprise me," Baba said with a nod. "Marge is quite skilled—well, more crazy than skilled—but skilled nonetheless."

Crap. This was a problem. Muted magic was incapacitating. Lesson? Maybe we did rely on magic too much. Marge might have a point. There had to be a way to find the damn cookie house. We could always fly around, but that could be as futile as walking. However...

"Can you conjure up some carbs?" I asked, getting excited.

"While I understand that you're pregnant, *Zelda*," Baba Yaga said, holding on to her patience with difficulty, "we really don't have time for a meal. I'd guess that Marge the douche nozzle is already aware of our presence. I believe finding the miserable old cow is more important than you stuffing your face."

"It's not for *me* to eat," I assured her. Although I figured I could throw back a few calories along with my half-assed plan. "It's for the carb-eating fairies."

"Once again?" Baba queried, confused.

"Carb. Eating. Fairies. It's how I found the house the first time," I told her. "They're these bizarre colorful little things that eat carbs. I think they speak French so I didn't understand a word they said, but the tiny weirdos led me to the cookie house."

She stared at me doubtfully—probably still thinking I was simply hungry and playing her for something sweet. I was—kind of, but it was the only idea I could come up with at the moment.

"Do you have a better plan?" I snapped.

"Surprisingly, no." Baba paced a large circle and then shrugged. "What do you like? Chocolate? Cookies? Cake? Candy?"

"Yes, yes, yes, and *yes*," I replied with a shudder of delight. Of course I could conjure it all up myself, but that would go against everything I'd promised Lucky and Charm. It was murky, but if someone else conjured it, I told myself taking a taste would be okay.

"Such a devious little witch," she said with a delighted laugh. "I'm well aware of your pledge to yourself about healthy eating. I'd suggest you only have a nibble of what I'm about to create."

"Whoa, whoa, whoa, can you read my mind?" I demanded a little freaked out. This was certainly unwelcome news. It was bad enough that Mac could sometimes hear my thoughts, but Baba Yaga? Not working for me.

"No, sadly I can't," she pouted. "That would be such a neat trick if I could. Save me years of time with interrogating wayward witches, but no. I had a little conversation with Lucky and Charm—they told me. Oh, and P.S. — those are awful names."

I was stunned to silence. She'd spoken to my babies? How in the Goddess's name did she speak to my babies without me knowing?

"They adore you and can't wait to pop into the world. Which by the way will be far sooner than you think," she replied with a mischievous little smile.

"They like me?" I whispered, touching my stomach and trying not to cry.

I failed.

"They love you," she corrected me, wiping a tear from my cheek. "They're good with Hildegard and Charles for middle names, but prefer Carol and Fabio for first names."

My stomach jumped in protest and I closed my eyes and giggled. Lucky and Charm were calling bullshit on Carol. I believed her on the middle names, but the first names? Not so much.

"Interesting," I said with a smirk and then I paused. "Wait. What exactly did you mean by giving birth sooner than I thought?"

"Look down," she insisted with a delighted laugh.

I did.

Oh. My. Goddess.

My stomach had grown in the short time we'd been wandering the berry patch. If I had to call it, I'd say I looked about six months along—or maybe more. Shit. I had no plans to squat in a field and birth my puppies.

"Did you do this?" I demanded, almost hysterical. "Is this your idea of a joke?"

"I did nothing of the sort," Baba huffed. "I believe it's the magic in the berry patch. I have no experience birthing babies, so I propose we get a move on, my dear."

"What about puppies?" I countered, still unconvinced Lucky and Charm were going to arrive in human form.

"No, Zelda. No experience in bringing puppies into the world either," she replied with a grin. "Let's bust a move and deal with the swamp-ass old biddy from hell."

With that lovely description, Baba Yaga waved her hands and created a pregnant witch's Nirvana—enough cookies, cakes, pies and candy to rot the teeth right out of your head. I clenched my hands at my sides and willed myself not to dive bomb the feast. It would be a clusterfuck if there were nothing left for the carb-eating fairies.

"How do we call the fairies?" she inquired, popping a cookie in her mouth.

119

"Do you speak French?" I asked, biting into a heavenly strawberry cupcake with butter cream icing.

"Languages are not my strongest skill," Baba admitted. "I know *merde* and *s'il vous plaît*."

"What does that mean?"

"*Merde* means shit and *s'il vous plait* means please."

"So you know how to politely ask them to take a crap?" I choked out with a laugh.

"It would appear so," Baba replied, grinning. "Not sure how helpful that's going to be."

"Stand back," I warned as I prepared myself. "I'll get the little flying freaks here."

Pinching off a piece of the light as air crust from a peach pie before I cast my spell, I almost forgot my name it was so delicious.

"Focus," Baba Yobossypants admonished. "Time is ticking and your belly is growing."

She was correct.

Shit.

"Goddess on high we're a little bit lost,

We need your assistance to avoid a steep cost.

Please send the freaky flying fuckers to aid our quest,

To restore the blessed harmony—we shall try out best."

Waving my hands in a circular motion, I waited for the Goddess to hear me.

Nothing happened.

Shit again.

"Freaky flying fuckers?" Baba Yaga questioned wryly. "That's the best you can do?"

"Look," I snapped at her. "I'm finding my mojo here. A little profanity seems to be a successful recipe for me, so can it."

And then the Goddess heard me. She heard me loud and clear—a little too loud and clear.

"Duck," I screeched as at least a hundred hungry carb-eating fairies descended on the buffet that Baba Yaga had conjured up. Every color of the rainbow was represented and then some, and the amount of flying glitter made me sneeze. I was sad to see they devoured all of the strawberry cupcakes and the pies disappeared in about three seconds flat. But they were here. That was all that mattered.

I hoped.

"Um... *s'il vous plaît* ... cookie house?" I shouted above the din of the eating frenzy.

I held a cookie up and drew a house in the air with my fingers. They ignored me.

"Coooo kieeee Hoooo uuuusssse," I repeated as a few observed me strangely.

"What in the ever loving hell?" Baba Yaga growled as she swatted at the aggressive little nightmares. "These deranged, eating things are going to help us?"

"Yes," I shouted as I pocketed a few chocolate chip cookies.

This was a clusterhump. How in the hell was I supposed to communicate with French- speaking carb eaters? Screw it. I knew what it was like to be obsessed with carbs and I knew how to get the attention of the mini flying bastards.

Not. A. Problem.

"Goddess on High, hear my call,

These flying shits have no manners at all.

Please trap all the goodies beneath magic cages,

No more for them until we are on the same, um... page—es."

"Seriously?" Baba shouted as she picked out a few fairies that had gotten trapped in her highly sprayed hair.

"It worked, didn't it," I yelled back as all the fairies froze in confusion and stared at the imprisoned treats.

"What now, brainiac?" Baba groused as she tried to repair her disastrous doo.

"Um... Fairies," I said using my outdoor brook no bullshit voice. "I no speaka Frencha, see voo play. Coooo kieeee Hooousssse? You take-a me there?"

I definitely had their attention, but they looked wildly perplexed.

"Don't you know any more French than *merde* and *s'il vous plaît*?" I asked Baba.

"Nope, but now you've gone and done it," she replied with wide eyes as she backed away from the impending shit show—pun intended.

"Nooooooooooooo!" I squeaked as one hundred little fairies whipped down their pants and prepared to take a dump. "NOOOOO *merde, s'il vous plaît s'il vous plaît s'il vous plaît*!!!"

"Draw a picture," Baba suggested, quickly handing me a marker and notebook she'd conveniently whipped up out of thin air.

"Good thinking," I said so relieved I wouldn't have to witness a massive fairy dump I almost cried.

I quickly drew a cookie house and a little old witch with a candy cane. I gave the witch bushy brows and for good measure I gave her a mustache and beard. The fairies floated around my head and watched intently. The aah's of recognition and the excited chattering made me exhale an enormous sigh of relief.

Like a school of colorful, insane fish they pointed the way and began to fly north.

"Did you bring your broom?" Baba joked as she took flight after the speedy fairies.

"Nope, don't need one," I replied with a giggle as I ran and launched myself into the air. "That shit's for fairy tales. This is real life."

One problem solved.

So many more to go.

Chapter 14

"Should we just walk up and knock?" Baba whispered as we hid in the bushes about three hundred feet from Marge's house.

The fairies had disappeared as soon as they had accomplished their mission. I was pretty sure they'd flown back to the buffet Baba had created to see if the cakes and cookies had been released from prison.

Baba's voice was unsteady and it made me queasy. Baba Yaga was *never* unsure of herself, and if she was, she typically hid it a hell of a lot better than she was doing today.

"What happened between you and Marge?" I asked her.

Going in blind was careless and stupid. I was going to be a mother for the Goddess's sake. My days of winging it were quickly coming to an end. Plus I needed to get back because Mac wanted a Ho Ho... not to mention I was getting more pregnant by the second. Carol was going to come clean or we were gonna hang out in the bushes all day and watch me give birth.

"It was her fault," she hissed. "It was awful and horrid and simply unforgivable."

"What was?" I asked.

Baba's brow wrinkled and she pressed her temples. Four times she started to speak and four times she stopped.

"No way," I muttered looking at her with narrow eyed surprise. "You have no clue why you hate Marge."

"It was hundreds of years ago," Baba Yaga sputtered indignantly. Little sparks flew from her fingertips and I was terrified she was going to set her lacquered hair on fire. "I can't be expected to remember everything. I mean, my Goddess, you try running the show for as many centuries as I have and see how much you remember, Little Missy."

"No thank you," I shot back, further convinced that the job of Baba Yaga wasn't for me.

"You have no choice. Neither did I," she said. "However, it comes with wonderful perks and having everyone kiss your ass and fear the ground you walk on is fun. Come on now... you know you'd like that."

"Is there a clothing allowance?" I asked.

"Of course there is. Look at me. Have you ever seen me in the same outfit twice?"

"Um... thankfully no," I muttered.

We needed a plan and we needed it now. It was shallow and ridiculous to be concerned about a clothing allowance for a job I didn't want. Shallow and ridiculous was the *old me*—well mostly. However, I was more alarmed that there was a clothing allowance considering what Baba Yotasteless wore on a regular basis.

I peeked out from behind the bush as I ran potential plans through my brain and screamed bloody murder.

"If I knew you were coming, I'd have baked a cake," Marge said, terrifying the living hoohoo out of me.

She stood there with compressed lips and a very unhappy expression on her wrinkly old face. Her bushy eyebrows were waggling a mile a minute and her fingers sparked ominously. Not good.

Of course my scream scared the living hell out of Baba Yaga, who hopped up and accidentally—*I think*—blew Marge's cookie house to smithereens. Marge then retaliated by wiggling her nose and dressing Carol in a frock from the Puritan era.

If I wasn't terrified that I might not live through the next few minutes, I would have cackled at the appalled expression on Baba Yaga's face as she examined the starched black sack she was now wearing.

Then it got really ugly.

With a wave of her hand, Carol zapped Marge bald. "I do not wear unflattering clothing, you smelly toad eater."

Not pleased, Marge gave Carol a huge hairy mole on the tip of her nose. "You're not welcome here, you brazen hooker from the underworld."

"*Charlatan*," Carol hissed.

"*Wand user*," Marge shouted.

"Take that back, you *potion sniffer*."

"*You* take that back, *Wicked Witch of the Worst*," Marge grunted, quite pleased with her insult.

I dove for cover and watched the debauchery unfold. They went at each other for a good ten minutes before they were both exhausted and very strange looking.

"Are you two idiots done?" I inquired.

"Not even close," Carol hissed as she waved her hands and gave Marge ears the size of an elephant.

Marge grabbed her head and shrieked at her new supersized aural units. Clearly not one to let something like receiving Dumbo ears go unpunished, she wiggled her fingers and increased the size of Baba's dainty feet to at least a size twenty-five. It was all kinds of wrong and I could see no end in sight. They were fairly unrecognizable now—ten more minutes and the nut bags would be horrifying.

However, it wasn't until I had what I could only guess was a gnarly and painful contraction that I was done. Playtime was over. I was clearly getting ready to blow out some puppies and I wanted to go home.

"Enough," I shouted, flinging my hands up and hanging both of the powerful witches in the air. "You two are behaving like possessed toddlers and I'm in labor for some fucked-up reason. We need to get this show on the road because I'm not squatting next to a demolished cookie house to give birth."

"Is she right in the head?" Marge asked Carol.

"No more than you or me," Carol answered.

I ignored the slights and went on.

"Marge, can you tell me what the problem is between you and Carol?"

Marge hung in the air like a pissed off marionette with monstrous ears and no hair. She just stared and gave me the evil eye.

"I thought so. Neither one of you knows why you hate each other. Right?"

Radio silence.

"Fine," I snapped. I wiggled my nose and undid all the damage they'd inflicted on each other. However, I dressed Carol a little more tastefully than she had been. I stayed with the eighties theme, but it was more Pat Benatar than Madonna. However, Marge was a shocker.

Gone was the little old lady and in her place was a gorgeous woman who looked disturbingly like Carol, but dressed a whole lot better. What the hey-hey? I stood in silence and gaped.

"What in the Goddess's name are you staring at, girlie?" Marge demanded.

"You," I choked out. "You're not old—you're beautiful."

"Wrong," Carol trilled. "She's at least a hundred years older than I am and I'm prettier. She's positively ancient."

"Pot, kettle, black," Marge sniped back. "And I'm only ninety-three years older, you snot nosed little magic abuser."

"Stop it," I shouted as I doubled forward with another contraction. "You two are worse than children. I've had about all I'm gonna put up with."

"Goddess on high, grant me this wish,

These witches are shitty, acting quite shrewish.

Take their power and hold it until they behave,

When they can be proper fucking witches, this spell you may waive."

A frigid breeze laced with a glittering silver mist blew through the berry patch and rendered the most powerful witch in existence—and possibly the second most powerful witch—magicless.

"Can she do that?" Marge hissed. "That spell was an abomination. Who ever heard of cursing to the Goddess?"

"The times they are a-changing," Carol said, also none too pleased to be without magic.

"She's *that* powerful?" Marge demanded angrily. "How is one so young who possesses dark magic so formidable?"

Baba Yaga fidgeted in the air for a few moments while I watched her brain working. With an enormous put upon sigh, she shrugged and shot Marge an unpleasant glare. "I don't see how it's any of your business, cow patty, since no one has seen or heard from you in centuries, but Zelda is my replacement."

"What?" Marge shrieked. "You have a *replacement*? Why don't I have a *replacement*?"

"Hang on here a minute," I cut in. "I've agreed to absolutely nothing. I'm a Shifter Wanker. I heal dumb asses."

"Yet you offered to heal me," Marge said sharply, giving me an eyeball that made me very happy she was presently without magic.

"If the shoe fits," Carol chimed in with an evil little giggle.

"Both of you are coming with me. We're going to sit down and work this shit out. And Marge, you have some explaining to do."

"Where exactly do you propose we sit down and chat?" Marge asked. "The Magical Menace blew my house up."

"Sorry about that," Carol apologized. "Really, I am. It was a knee jerk reaction."

Leaving them hanging in the air, I stomped over the pile of cookie rubble and examined it. Baba Yaga had done a thorough job—even the crumbs looked like dust—only a few cookie chunks here and there. Gooey bits of gumdrops oozed everywhere. Green and messy. I didn't remember all the gumdrops on the roof being green, but clearly they had to have been. I'd been so obsessed with the chocolate door that I supposed I'd overlooked the all green roof—green and goopy.

Wait one motherhumpin' minute...

My gut clenched, but this time it wasn't a contraction. Nope, not even close.

Something was very, very wrong here.

Green goop? Oozing green goop...

My body froze and my brain started working over time. Chills skittered up my spine and I silently thanked the Goddess for giving me the forethought to ban Marge's magic. Visions of the deadly syringe filled with the gooey green potion filled my head. I'd found it. I'd found the source of the lurking fucking evil. Marge was the creator of it, I was in labor, and I'd just made sure Baba Yaga had no magic.

Shitshitshitshit.

"Lucky and Charm, close your eyes and stay in my tummy for at least another couple of hours. I have some business to take care of and I want your Daddy to be with me when you guys arrive. If I have to blow you out, he has to pay for knocking me up. That's probably TMI, but I want to have an open and honest relationship with you guys. Can you do that for Mommy?" I whispered, gently rubbing my stomach.

A ticklish wave darted around my stomach and I knew my babies had heard me—I just hoped they obeyed. I let a grateful smile pull at my lips, but only briefly. My children were going to enter a world without the lurking fucking evil in it. The end was in reach and we were definitely on the last chapter of this unfortunate fairy tale.

Turning away from the wreckage of the house, I marched over to Marge and slashed my hands through the air. She was now bound, gagged and confined in a cage.

"You," I hissed in a fury. My body shook with rage as the images of my aunt's death raced across my vision. "You made the evil that killed my Aunt Hildy. You're the reason the honey badgers were able to take her magic. Which then in turn made me have to take my mother's magic from her. I possess dark magic because of *you*."

"Um… Zelda," Baba Yaga interrupted.

"Not now, Carol. I've got this."

"You're sure about that?" she asked.

"Damn right," I snapped. "Stay out of it."

"Will do."

Flicking my fingers I released Baba from the air and restored her magic. She dropped to the ground with an unladylike thud and grunt, but she was free. My finesse wasn't outstanding, but my intentions were good. I didn't need my mentor, but she didn't need to be helpless. Just in case Marge had more evil up her sleeve, I didn't want the insane woman I secretly adored unable to defend herself.

Maybe my ego had grown along with my stomach, but I was going with it. I had a limited amount of time to save the world and I really wanted to give birth in Assjacket with my doula DeeDee at my side.

"Do you want to explain yourself?" I growled at a wide-eyed Marge.

"Um… Zelda," Baba Yaga cut in with a politely raised hand.

"Yes?" I asked, exasperated.

"She's gagged. Don't think she can answer you."

"Right," I said, slapping my forehead and wiggling my nose.

The duct tape ripped from Marge's mouth and she cried out in pain. My instinct was to comfort her. What the hell was wrong with me? She'd made a potion that stole magic and killed witches. She didn't deserve my compassion. Goddess, being happy and in love had made me soft.

"Start talking, Marge," I instructed tightly.

"Nuclear energy," Marge replied flatly.

"You're cryptic horse poop isn't going to save you," I threatened.

"I certainly hope not," she said, watching me with interest. "However, I'd think you'd enjoy something a bit wicked—being as dark as you are."

"You thought wrong," I shot back.

"Kill me girl. Do it now. It will save me from having to do it myself."

Her lips were bleeding where the tape had torn itself away. My fingers itched to heal her, but I held myself back. Reminding myself that my aunt had pled for her life because of the lurking fucking evil Marge had created, I made myself watch her bleed. Her comfort was not my problem.

Shit, yes it was.

I slapped my forehead.

No. No, it wasn't.

Pacing back and forth like a lunatic while I silently argued with myself was wearing me out. What exactly was I going to do here?

Wing it. I was going to wing it. NO. I was going to be a mom in a few hours. Moms didn't wing things with enormous ramifications. I mean my mom did, but that's why I was a mess with a porno loving rabbit Shifter for a therapist. Marge needed to confess and then I would punish her… but I wasn't the Goddess.

I was just Zelda the Witch who was a barely passable Shifter Whisperer. Who was I to punish her for her evil deeds?

"Marge, I'm having a bit of a Jiminy Cricket moment here. I'm going to ask you nicely to explain yourself because I'm pretty sure Lucky and Charm can hear everything I say. Yes, I may possess dark magic, but it wasn't my choice to have it. I've mostly got a handle on it, but if you push me far enough, it's anyone's guess how I'll use it. You wanting me to kill you is either brilliant reverse psychology or you're crazier than I thought. Tell me why you created something so evil. Make me understand. Please."

"It's all in how you use it, girlie," she said wearily.

I glanced behind and noted that Baba Yaga stood quietly, watching Marge with great interest.

"Like nuclear energy?" I asked slowly.

"Yes. I stopped last week."

"Stopped what?" Baba Yaga asked.

"I thought the unbalanced red head was in charge here, *Carol*," Marge said.

"She is," Carol said at the very same time I uttered, "I'm not."

I looked at the witch I considered my superior in every way. Then I looked at them both.

"And I'm not unbalanced," I added for good measure.

Both of the women shot me a disbelieving glance.

"Fine, I'm unbalanced, but I don't create potions that kill witches."

"Whatever," Marge said. "Either or both of you can kill me. I'm tired and I'm done."

"Oh Marge, no," Baba Yaga whispered sadly.

Now I was just confused. This wasn't going quite like it was supposed to—whatever the heck that even meant. Marge was tired. What in the Goddess's name was Marge tired *of*? And why was Baba sad at the thought of destroying the source of the lurking fucking evil?

"Have you muted the magic in the world?" I asked, deciding to get as many questions answered as I could, since I wasn't sure what was happening.

"Nuclear energy," she repeated.

Inhaling deeply and blowing it out slowly through my lips, I pressed my twitching hands to my sides. It wouldn't do any good at all to zap her. I'd just feel awful. There were far too many puzzle pieces missing to pass judgment at this point.

"Can't you be a bit more forthcoming?"

"I can," a horrifyingly familiar male voice said as he materialized next to Marge's cage.

Bermangoogleshitz smelled like shit on a stick. His beady eyes were as black as night and his hair matched. As the acrid green smoke around him dissipated, I noticed his horns had grown. Lovely.

"How did you get in here, you horrible piece of magical trash?" Marge hissed, backing into the corner of her cage. "No one summoned you."

I watched, fascinated as Baba Yaga sprinted to the cage, reached through the bars, and placed her hand on Marge in solidarity. Confusion was mild for what I was experiencing now. Why in the world was Bermangoogleshitz here? And why was Carol protecting Marge?

"Interesting you should ask, Marge," Bermangoogleshitz sneered. "Somehow the wards fell down around this delightful wrinkle that I've been banned from for centuries. Imagine my excitement at the thought of being welcomed. I've missed you, lovely Marge."

"You're not welcome here," Carol ground out through clenched teeth, wiggling her fingers and covertly freeing Marge from the ropes she was bound in.

"Ahhhhhh, the great Baba Yaga and her exquisite sister," Bermangoogleshitz said with so much derision it practically dripped from his forked tongue. "It's been ages since we were all together. Pity. Think of all the fun we missed over the years."

Holy shitballs, Carol and Marge were *sisters*? I scratched my head and stared at them.

"State your business," Marge snapped in a voice that scared the heck out of me.

"I want the potion," he replied.

"Over my dead body," she hissed.

"That can be arranged, my dear. And the pleasure would be all mine."

And for better or worse, that's when I stepped in...

Chapter 15

"Not happening, Bermangooglesnot," I shouted, as I pushed him back with a shot of dark magic and stood between him and the cage. "It's mine. I found it first."

"Why you're more evil than I'd originally thought," he purred, nodding in approval. "So you want to own the world as well. Interesting."

The lie had slipped from my mouth easily. I didn't want to own the world at all. I wanted to have my babies, some Ho Hos, and live happily ever after with Mac. Owning the world was nowhere on my list. However, Bermangoogleshitballs owning the world wasn't going to happen on my clock. I'd fight him for Marge's nuclear energy potion and then I'd get to the bottom of Marge...

"Yes. I mean, who wouldn't want to own the world," I spat sarcastically. "It's mine, so leave."

"Make me."

"What are you? Five?" I yelled. I'd already dealt with two adults behaving like children. I was in no mood to deal with another. And I was getting dangerously close to blowing my own children out.

"Hardly," he shot back in his oily voice. "You're weak. You won't use it correctly."

What in the Goddess's name was he babbling about? Details would have been nice, but I was vaguely cognizant of the overall picture here, and the evil bastard could under no circumstance have the green goop. I'd figure out the rest later.

Lucky and Charm moved in my stomach and it took everything I had not to gasp or scream. A power very dark began to swirl inside me. I did my best to shield my children from it, but soon realized they were part of the source.

My world tilted on its axis for a brief and horrid second as I realized I'd passed on my dark magic to the lives inside me. It sickened me. My children were going to have to fight the very same fight I had to deal with.

My rage at Marge increased and my hatred for Bermangooglejackhole consumed me. If my son was born with horns, I was going to poop a watermelon.

"*It's okay Mommy,*" a little voice inside my head promised.

"*You use dark against dark to protect the light,*" the other voice whispered.

Oh my Goddess. I was having a conversation with Lucky and Charm. There were a million things I wanted to say, but time was ticking and the heinous warlock was observing me closely.

"*You're not dark?*" I asked them, keeping my face neutral and staring hard at Bermangooglecrap.

"*Only a little,*" my baby girl assured me. "*The Goddess gave us this gift so we can make the world better.*"

"*It is only a small part of who we will be,*" my son said. "*We're mostly love, because we were created in love.*"

"*Can I ask a weird question?*" I inquired.

"*Yes.*"

"Are you guys going to come out speaking full sentences? Cause that's a little weird. Not that I wouldn't be okay with it, but a little forewarning might be nice for your dad."

"We will be typical babies—kind of," my boy said with an adorable giggle.

Hmmmm… so many questions and so little time.

"Can you guys hold off on your first entrance until I'm done here?" I asked, deciding not to probe into the *kind of* comment right now. If my boy had horns I would love him anyway.

"Yep! Maybe you should get back to business. The bad guy seems to be losing patience."

"I'm on it," I told them. *"You two just hang tight. Mommy can handle Bermangoogleshitforbrains."*

"Can we give you a piece of information that might be helpful?" my little boy asked.

"Yep."

"Bermangooglebutthead is Sassy's father."

"You're shitting me," I gasped.

"Nope not yet. Baba Yaga told us that. Didn't know why, but now we do."

"Getting bored here," Bermangoogleshitz said with an eye roll.

"Sorry about that," I replied, searching his face and trying to find a resemblance to my idiot best friend. Thankfully there was none. He was one ugly motherhumper.

"We might have a little problem here," I said, developing my plan as I spoke.

So much for not winging it.

"You got through the wrinkle on a technicality. The ward was broken by me—not Marge. So if you take anything, you're breaking the seven hundredth magical commandment."

I felt Marge and Carol's eyes boring into the back of my head, and if I wasn't mistaken, I was fairly certain I heard Marge stifle a giggle. I knew I was pulling a doozy out of my rear end, but if I could avoid a smackdown that I might not win, we'd all be better off.

"Like I would care about the seven hundredth magical commandment?" he snarled as slithery black serpents appeared around his feet. He walked toward the remains of the house and produced a glass vial in his hand. His smile was vicious and the darkness inside me begged to come out and play.

"You're making a mistake, jack-hole," I said pleasantly with a friendly wave.

My tone stopped him and he turned back to me and laughed. "You're nothing—not good enough and definitely not evil enough. I'm taking the potion. Your choice is to stop me or not. But I will promise you, little *pregnant* witch, it will not be pleasant for you or your children if you try."

"The seven hundredth commandment bars you from ever seeing your daughter."

He stared at me like I'd grown horns and I was almost sure that a heart wrenching sadness washed over his features for a split second. Did the evil bastard have feelings? Doubtful... probably gas.

"Did you even know you had one? Probably not—smelly deadbeat dads with horns and pet snakes usually suck. But anyhoo, it states clearly that if you break a pentagramius de jure merde de novo rule from the book of ancient spells—you forfeit all magically legal claims to any heir you might have unfortunately sired. You see, Bermangoogledork, I *might* just know who she is. You certainly don't deserve her, but if you take the potion, you will NEVER have the chance know her at all. I'll kill her to make sure of it," I ground out, lying through my teeth about the killing part. The thought of my killing Sassy was so ludicrous I almost laughed, but bit it back with effort. However, if I was going to fight dark with dark, that was as evil as you could get.

"Did you say shit in French?" Bermangoogleshitz questioned, mightily confused.

"I most certainly did not, you crotch jockey."

"I believe you did."

"Maybe you're just smelling your upper lip," I snapped. *Did I say shit in French?* I might have. Stringing bogus lawyerly sounding words together was difficult.

His response was a laugh—oily, ugly and pure evil.

I wanted to smite his ass straight to hell for threatening my babies, and I wanted to hurt him badly for being Sassy's father. He could threaten me till the cows came home, but he was treading on dangerously thin ice speaking about my children.

Assholes like him didn't deserve to be anyone's father. Honestly, I hoped I had said shit. It was fitting since he was a piece of it.

His roar hurt my eardrums and echoed through my head. "I call bullshit on all of that. I've never heard of the book of ancient spells. You're making all of this up, witch."

His stance was frightening, but I caught the quick glimpse of something that looked like hope in his beady eyes. Watching him war with himself was disconcerting. I worried that I'd gone too far so I let my dark magic roam free inside me. If I had to take him out, I was going to go out fighting with all I had.

"Possibly," I agreed with a shrug that I prayed appeared casual. "But are you *sure* I'm making it up?"

I heard Baba Yaga's quick intake of breath behind me. Right then it dawned on me that I was the only one present who could take Bermangoogleshitz on. Dark had to fight dark. Right now, I was very dark and very scared that the bastard would call my partial bluff.

Fighting Bermangoogleshitz was not a sure win—not even close.

He glanced down at the vial in his hands and a rueful smile pulled at his thin lips. The horrid looking man gazed at me long and hard. I stood my ground and glared back. My instinct was to run like hell, but far too much was at stake. After what felt like an eternity, he laughed—and again it wasn't pretty.

Dropping the vial to the ground, he crushed the glass beneath his foot. The sound of breaking glass was sickeningly ominous—just like the man. His snakes slithered up his body and hissed at me menacingly. Bermangoogleshitz was a horror movie come to life. Truth be told, I had no intention of bringing him into Sassy's life. She drove me bonkers, but I secretly adored her, and would bust down on anyone who meant her harm.

"If I find out you're lying, I will come back to you when you least expect it, and destroy everything you love. Are we clear?" he asked so calmly I almost turned and ran.

"We are. Get your sorry stinky ass out of the wrinkle. You're not welcome here and never will be."

"We shall meet again, Zelda—very soon."

In an explosion of putrid green smoke, the monster disappeared and I fell to my knees in relief. But what had I done? In trying to save the world, had I thrown Sassy under the bus? The bile rose in my throat and all I wanted to do was curl into a ball and cry.

"Zelda," Baba Yaga whispered as she knelt beside me and stroked my hair. "You were brilliant."

"No, I fucked up," I blubbered. "I've outed Sassy—said I would kill her. I mean I didn't say her name, but the fucker knows he has a daughter now. This is horrible. I need to have the puppies and then go kill that bastard so he won't hurt Sassy. She's an idiot, but she's *my* idiot. I can't let that disgusting piece of crap near her. He'll eat her alive."

Baba Yaga's amused chuckle pissed me off. I wondered if she had any friends at all. She was heartless.

"It's not funny, Carol," I shouted at her, wiping my nose on my sleeve. "Sassy's mother was heinous—dropped her off at an orphanage when she was a little girl—and never came back. And now she gets to find out her father is a stank-ass evil warlock with horns? Nothing about this is fucking funny."

"Sassy is far stronger than you think. She has a right to know her father," Baba Yaga said, ignoring my disrespect. "However, she shall not go to him unprotected or unprepared. You will be there for her."

"You got that right," I huffed. "Most of the time I want to throat punch her, but if that fucker lays one hand on her in violence, I'll kill him where he stands."

"She's an odd one," Marge said, stepping up behind her *sister* and looking at me as if I were a science experiment.

"Yes, well aren't we all?" Baba Yaga replied to her sister, squeezing her hand.

"And you," I ground out, getting to my feet and poking Marge in the chest. "You and your nuclear witchy energy... "

I stopped and stared at her open mouthed. *Made for good... but used for evil.*

Bermangoogleshitz wanted that potion badly—wanted to own the world. Marge was tired. She wanted to stop. Had she created the potion for good and it had blown up in her face because of people like Bermangoogleshitz, my mother and the honey badgers? Had the evil outweighed the good? She said the nuclear energy had muted the magic... or was it the lack thereof? Did it also create magic?

The two witches watched me and waited.

Magic was *our* nuclear energy. The very potion that kept the magical balance, in the wrong hands, could destroy it.

"Tough shit if you're tired, Marge. You have a job to do. Not everyone is a Bermangooglehole, or a honey badger, or my mother. Most of us are good—or trying to be."

"I think she's beginning to get it," Baba Yaga said proudly as she looked at me.

"Took her long enough. Actually thought she might kill me for a few minutes there," Marge said with a grin.

"I still might," I informed her, waving my hands and restoring her magic. "Was this a fucking test?"

"Not really, no. However, if it had been you passed with flying colors," Baba Yaga said, with an unapologetic shrug. "I'd love to say I planned it, but I didn't. I might have had a bit of an idea what the problem was, but I wasn't sure. Marge has been in hiding for centuries."

"Why?" I asked Marge, who actually did look really tired.

"Why do you think?" she countered.

"I think you naively made the green goop for good, but in the wrong hands it's devastating."

Marge snapped her fingers and her cookie house reappeared in a blast of powdered sugar and sprinkles. "Come with me," she instructed as she walked back into her house.

"Is it safe?" I whispered to Baba Yaga.

"Yes, dear. Marge is a gaping asshole, but she really is truly good."

"I heard that, Carol," Marge yelled.

"Come on," Baba Yaga urged as she followed her sister into the cookie house. "There's a bit more you need to learn."

"Bout to drop some puppies here," I warned.

"No worries. This won't take long."

Famous last words.

Chapter 16

"Wait, so you knew all along that the lurking fucking evil was actually the substance that created pure light magic?" I shouted at Baba Yaga as she sat on the couch and munched on a snickerdoodle.

"Yes."

"You suck," I told her, as I pocketed a handful of dark chocolate covered almonds to eat when I gave birth later today. "You told me I had to find the lurking fucking evil and keep the balance in Assjacket."

"Correct," Baba Yaga replied.

"You are so full of shit, Carol."

"You got that one right," Marge said, trying to bribe me over to her side by handing me a homemade strawberry milkshake with an obscene amount of whipped cream on top.

Okay. It worked.

"Actually, I'm an outstanding multi-tasker," Baba Yaga countered. "You'll see one day yourself, Zelda. Presiding over all the witches in the world is a pain in the ass. You'll eventually inherit the job and I'll go on a long overdue vacation. Your training started the day I sentenced you to prison. I needed to keep an eye on you."

"So you knew Fabio was still alive? You knew I didn't run over him on purpose—that I didn't kill him?"

She nodded and smirked. "Of course. However, the *not on purpose* part is somewhat debatable. And let's not forget your irresponsible use of magic."

"Whatever," I snapped. I was still mulling over the fact I'd spent nine months in the pokey as a *mostly* innocent witch. There was no doubt I was a better person for it, but admitting it wasn't going to happen any time soon.

Baba Yaga continued as she watched me stew. "So I assumed Marge had created a wrinkle in this area when I realized what had been used to kill our beloved Hildy. I was also aware that no harm would come to you if you found the crazy old bat. She's worked very hard to stay hidden from me, but she didn't know you. You had a far better chance of finding her than I did."

"And you two are sisters?"

"Yep—little known fact and we like it that way," Marge admitted with an eye roll and a huff. "We're both creators. Carol was meant to lead and I was meant to create and spread a magical balance in the world."

"How's that working out?" I asked rudely.

Marge's laugh was so reminiscent of Baba Yaga's that I almost smiled—almost. I wasn't ready to play nice yet.

"Not well, girlie. Tell me how you see it," she prodded.

I thought about it for a minute and then sighed. "Magic—specifically your green goop—is our nuclear energy. Made with good intentions, but can be used for evil in the wrong hands."

"She's smart," Marge told Carol approvingly before looking at me. "You are correct. When the Goddess gave me the ability to create the potion she didn't include the fine print. For centuries, I lived in the open and was worshipped for my gift. All I had to do was spread minuscule amounts around and everything was perfect. It was intoxicating. However there's always a dark underbelly to most silver linings. Power can lead to a false sense of invincibility."

"I never knew how you did it," Baba Yaga said quietly. "I was always jealous of what you could do. And then you disappeared and I couldn't find you. I thought you were dead."

"I'm truly sorry," Marge whispered, staring at her sister with tears in her eyes. "I'm paying a penance to the Goddess for revealing the secret potion to the wrong person."

"You told him?" Baba asked, surprised.

"Yes," she admitted. "I told him what I did, but thankfully not the recipe."

"Why?" Baba questioned.

"Because I loved him and because he asked."

Oh my hell, a few more details would have been awesome, but interrupting their moment would be beyond wrong—even I knew that. It was difficult, but I stayed silent. Downing the strawberry milkshake helped. It was hard to butt in with a mouthful of ice cream. They went on as if I wasn't here.

Marge sat down next to her sister and took her hands in her own. "There's a reason I never shared exactly what I did or how I did it. It's too dangerous for those who know, but youth breeds arrogance and my ego got the better of me—or rather Bermangoogleshitz got the better of me. After that I went into hiding."

"Whoa," I choked out, spitting milkshake everywhere. "Please tell me you did not do the nasty with Bermangooglegrossmeout—he was the guy you loved?"

"He was quite beautiful until he fell too deeply into the dark," Marge admitted with a shrug. "I thought I was in love and I thought he could be trusted. Two very large mistakes that I must live with."

It was all starting to add up, but not quite.

"He did some bad shit with the green goop?" I asked with a shudder.

Marge closed her eyes and nodded. "Very bad. Ultimately it was my fault because I shared my secret with him. Seclusion from all whom I loved was the price I had to pay."

"How in the hell did the honey badgers and my mother end up with the potion if you've been in hiding?"

Baba Yaga stroked her sister's hair as if she were trying to memorize it and waited. Marge closed her eyes and let her head fall back on her shoulders.

"I was lonely," Marge whispered. "My self-imprisonment was making me insane. Around seventy-five years ago, I began to let Shifters into my berry patch so I could at least have some interaction with people, although it was from a distance. The Goddess made that concession for me."

"And witches?" I asked.

"No, the patch is warded against witches," she explained.

"Um... I call bullshit. I got in, Fabio got in, and Sassy got in. And my mother must have gotten in."

Marge titled her head in thought and her eyes squinted in confusion. "Your mother never set foot in my wrinkle, she must have gotten the potion from the honey badgers. You, my dear, can pass through any ward as you're set to be the next Baba Yaga. The Goddess knew that Fabio was in the area and let him pass, but who is this Sassy? Is she a healer witch?"

"Nope," Baba Yaga said with a giggle. "Not a healer— definitely not a healer."

"She's my fucking magical menace, clothes stealing, big-boobed nightmare of a best friend," I explained. "I have no clue why she got through your ward. She's not exactly big in the brains department… "

"My, that sounds familiar," Baba Yaga said giving her sister the side eye.

"Well, it's a mystery then," Marge said wearily, gently elbowing her sister. "However, I decided that I was done until the Goddess paid me a rather unsettling visit last night. She took me on a little trip to show me what the lack of magical balance was doing to our world."

"Which is why you made another batch?" I asked.

"Yes," she agreed slowly. "However, I want out. I can't live like this anymore."

"Why the old lady in the cookie house disguise?" Baba Yaga inquired. "I mean I know you always loved to bake, but an *old lady*? You're as vain as Zelda is."

"Excuse me?" I hissed, giving the eighties reject the evil eye.

"Fine," Baba Yaga caved with a laugh. "I too am very cognizant of my appearance."

"The old woman amused me," Marge replied. "I could take no chance of being recognized for who I really was."

"The secret's kind of out now," I said, feeling bad for her.

"Yes, well I suppose I'll have to create another wrinkle in time somewhere far, far away. However, the Goddess has given my back my privilege to occasionally see the ones I love," Marge said with a smile on her face that didn't reach her sad eyes. "Duty is duty."

This was awful. Marge was actually one of the most important pieces of our magical puzzle. Why should she have to live in seclusion?

"Maybe not. I might have a solution," Baba Yaga said, thinking aloud with an enormous grin pulling at her lips.

Her delight was contagious, but I cringed at whatever plan she was brewing. Most of her wild hairs were horrifying. As long as it didn't involve me going back to the pokey, I supposed it would be okay.

"Really?" Marge asked, perking up with wide eyes and a hopeful expression.

"Um… guys," I gasped out as my stomach went as hard as a rock and the pain left me breathless. "I think we have a little issue here."

"Dear Goddess," Marge shrieked, getting up and running around her small house. "She's about to have the babies. I'm clueless about this."

"Shit," Baba shouted. "I'm worthless too. Um… get hot water and soft music and maybe some diapers and a teddy bear and maybe something alcoholic for us."

"On it." Marge waved her hands in a panic and the small house suddenly filled with stuffed animals as elevator music wafted through the room at concert decibels.

"Not working," I grunted, as I swatted at the mountain of teddy bears. "No room at the inn to actually blow the puppies out."

"Damn it, get rid of the bears Marge... and that music sucks. Try some Madonna. Zelda's having little Werewolves anyway. Conjure up some wolves," Baba Yaga ordered, all in one hysterical breath.

"Real ones?" Marge asked for clarification.

"Goddess, *NO*, you dingbat! That would be a clusterfuck."

"STOP," I shouted at both of them. "I want Mac and I want my dad. Is the ward still down?"

Marge waved her hands wildly. "It is now. Where are they?"

"The whole town was going to surround the perimeter of the berry patch," I grunted out during a contraction that made me see stars.

"Perfect," Marge shouted. "Take my hand, Carol. We're bringing everyone here."

"Now?" Baba Yaga asked, grabbing onto her sister.

"Yes. Right now!"

And with the combined power of two of the strongest witches in existence, the entire population of Assjacket was hurtled through the sky in a cookie-scented tornado. The landing thuds sounded like it was storming cats and dogs—or rather wolves, rabbits, raccoons, deer, lions, beavers and then some. But they were all here.

And we were all about to meet the newest members of our community.

I just had to get through blowing them out first.

Chapter 17

"Does anyone but me find this a bit odd?" Fabio asked in an utter state of shock as he ran his hands nervously through his hair. "I mean her stomach was flat this morning."

"Can it, Fabdudio," I growled as I tried desperately to find a position that wasn't horrifically painful.

"Nature is beautiful," Marge said reverently, elbowing my dad who was about to say something else probably equally as unhelpful.

"Dear Goddess, Fabio," Baba Yaga whispered, paling considerably as she observed me writhing around on Marge's guest room bed and zapping magic at whoever was in my sightline. "We are never having children. Ever."

"Fine by me," Fabio agreed, ducking a rather aggressive bolt I flung at him.

"Zelda, maybe you should just toughen up a bit. It'll be over in a jiffy if you keep a stiff upper lip," Fabio explained with a fatherly smile, trying to find something positive and helpful to say.

He failed.

Thankfully all of my friends and neighbors were outside of the cookie house and didn't see me turn my father into a toad for suggesting something so ridiculous.

Mac, DeeDee, Baba Yaga and Marge were quick learners and avoided saying any trite bullshit sure to set me off.

"Get the puppies out... get them out now," I screamed through a particularly horrible contraction. I wanted to castrate Mac and kick the serene expression off of DeeDee's face. "NOW."

"They're coming, Zelda," DeeDee said calmly, mopping my face and trying to make me comfortable.

There was no making me comfortable. I opened my eyes after thinking I'd died and gone on to the Next Adventure to find that my dad was once again my dad. However, Baba Yaga had wisely covered his mouth with duct tape.

"You're doing great, baby," Mac said, wincing ever so slightly at the death grip I had on his hand.

"You are *never* putting Bon Jovi in me again," I ground out as another contraction came over me. "When I'm done here, I'm going to neuter you."

"That's fine, sweetie," Mac said lovingly as he gently pushed my sweaty hair out of my face.

"Are you even listening to me? AHHHHHHHHH," I screamed as I was now beyond sure that watermelons were not supposed to pass through openings meant for Bon Jovis.

"We're getting close," DeeDee said with an excited smile.

"What in the Goddess's name do you mean *we*?" I grunted as I tried to do the breathing crap she'd taught me. Mac was breathing with me and winning by a long shot. "I don't see anyone but me trying to blow a tractor-trailer out of my hoohoo."

"Soon, baby. Just hold on," Mac whispered, pressing his lips to my forehead.

"I've changed my mind," I screeched as my stomach locked up tighter than the pokey I'd spent nine months in. "Let's just leave them in there. It's fine. They like it in there."

"Nature is beautiful," Marge said, only seconds before I zapped her ass, *hard*.

"Nature sucks," I informed her in a brief respite from contractions. "And while we all experiencing *nature* at my freakin' expense, I'd prefer not to have my dad in the room while I'm buck ass naked, spread eagle, and about to blow some people out of my woowoo. If you're staying Fabio, you need to come to the top of the bed."

"Will he be in danger up there?" Baba Yaga asked, which I thought was a pretty reasonable question.

"Yes. Yes he will."

"Alrighty then," she said with a winning smile and a thumbs up. "We'll just wait outside until you're done."

"Right behind you," Marge called out as she sprinted after the quickly retreating couple.

There was blessed silence in the room and I took a few deep breaths preparing myself for the next round of hell.

"I can't do this," I whispered to Mac.

"You can," he promised. "You are so very beautiful and strong. You humble me, my love."

"Sorry about the neuter thing," I said. "I didn't mean it—well, I did at the time, but right now you're safe. I'm really quite fond of your Bon Jovi. I can't promise I won't change my mind in the next five minutes, but I love you and your Bon Jovi."

"I love you too, little witch." Mac laughed and kissed me again.

"Zelda, it's time to push," DeeDee said in her ever calm voice. "Are you ready?"

"Do I have a choice?"

"Nope," she shot back with a smile.

"Then let's blow out some puppies."

"That's my girl," Mac said.

Amazingly the pushing was the easiest part. It only took ten minutes of me swearing like a sailor and threatening to remove Mac's Bon Jovi with a dull butter knife before my children entered the world—one right after the other. Mac was an emotional wreck and DeeDee was as calm as a cucumber. And me? I was amazing. Magic had nothing on the miracle of birth.

"Are they furry?" I asked frantically as Mac cut the cords and DeeDee cleaned the babies up.

"Nope," she sang out as she swaddled my crying children with great care.

"Horns?" I demanded weakly. I was beyond exhausted.

"No horns, Zelda. They're perfect." Mac said with tears in his gorgeous eyes as he held a bundle of pink and a bundle of blue.

It was all kinds of sexy that my beautiful alpha wolf was so moved by the birth of our children.

"Can I see them?" I whispered, terrified of what I'd discover.

I was certain they loved me when they were hitching a ride in my tummy, but now that they were here, would they feel the same way?

Mac gently laid our babies on my chest. My heart was pounding so loudly I was certain everyone could hear it. Soft curly tufts of red hair dusted two perfect little heads. Sapphire blue eyes that matched their father's and smiles all their own beamed at me.

My breath caught in my throat and tears filled my eyes. Words were impossible. There were none perfect enough to describe my babies. A fierce wave of love consumed me and I silently promised Lucky and Charm I would defend them with my life until the day I moved on to the Next Adventure. I loved Mac with everything that I was, but this was different somehow. It felt life changing and important and really, really wonderful.

"I think they like me," I whispered, tracing my daughter's Cupid's bow mouth and gently cupping my son's chubby cheek.

"They love you just like I do," Mac said as he lay down next to me and ran his hands carefully and lovingly over our children.

"We made them," I said with a giggle, staring at the tiny people with wonder.

"And I think you did a pretty good job," DeeDee said as she finished cleaning me up and tucked a blanket over my little family and me. "I'll leave you alone for a bit so you four can get acquainted. When you're ready for visitors, just call out."

"Thank you, DeeDee," I said with an enormous smile that I couldn't contain.

"The pleasure was all mine, Zelda," she said, quietly slipping from the room.

"Are we still calling them Lucky and Charm?" Mac inquired with a lopsided smile.

"In my head I am, but we're gonna have to come up with something better than that." I brushed my lips over their soft foreheads and breathed in their beautiful baby scent.

I was exhausted but strangely wired. I'd never felt so alive or powerful in all my thirty years.

"Were you kind of shocked that they came today?" I asked Mac with a yawn.

"You could say that." He chuckled and gathered the three of us in his arms. "You were four weeks pregnant when we woke up this morning."

"I'm pretty shocked too. It was the magic in the berry patch that sped things up."

"Speaking of, the magic in the area has been restored. Was it Marge?"

"Yes and it's a long and weird story. Can we take a nap and I'll tell you everything later?"

"Yep," he said as he plumped the pillow behind my head and tucked my hair behind my ears. "You sleep and I'll watch over you and the babies."

"Okay," I said as my heavy lids fluttered closed.

"Thank you, Zelda," he whispered as I let sleep overtake me. "You have given me more than I ever dreamed of. With you, I have a life worth living."

"Love you," I mumbled.

"Love you more."

"Not possible."

"Oh, but it is, my little witch. You have no idea how possible it is."

I fell asleep with everything I needed in this world surrounding me. I was loved and I loved right back. Mac might think he loved me more, but I knew the truth. I loved him just as much as he loved me and we both adored our children more than words could ever express.

***

Later the room was packed with my friends and family. I'd napped with my babies for an hour and then Mac held them while I showered and got dressed in the fabulous green Prada dressing gown Fabdudio had surprised me with. Of course he'd also had the wherewithal to buy matching Prada baby outfits for Lucky and Charm. We were quite the spiffy picture.

"Oh. My. Goddess," Sassy said knocking my fat cats off the bed and sniffing the babies. "I want one of these so bad."

"You can't have mine and you are *not* allowed to borrow them," I told her sternly. My clothes were one thing, but my babies were entirely another.

"Can I babysit?"

Pressing my lips together so I didn't shout something rude that I'd regret, I nodded. "When they get a little older. Right now, they're all mine."

"And mine," Mac added with a grin so proud, I giggled.

"Shifter twins are very rare," Wanda said as she and little Bo marveled at the tiny bundles.

"As are witch twins," Baba Yaga added, not wanting the other half of the twins' heritage left out. "The Goddess has truly blessed you, my child."

Looking around the room, I felt ridiculously blessed. Roger, Bob and Simon were loaded down with all sorts of baby toys. Chad, Chip, Chunk and Chutney had thoughtfully—or thoughtlessly—brought my toothless babies who couldn't even eat food yet, a large case of chewing gum. Fat Bastard, Jango Fett and Boba Fett arrived with adorable tiny bibs and a baby sized cans of spray paint. Of course the spray paint was going back to wherever they stole it from, but I reminded myself it was the thought that counted.

Baba Yaga and Marge had conjured up tiny wands and brooms for the babies and Jeeves came bearing food—tons of delicious food that he'd apparently whipped up in Marge's kitchen. My people were eating and drinking and cooing over the newest additions to our tight little community. It was all kinds of wonderful.

"Have you named them yet?" DeeDee asked.

I looked at Mac and grinned. While I'd showered, I'd explained what had happened—everything that had happened including the identity of Sassy's father. He listened with a tense expression and asked plenty of questions. I knew he hated that my job put me in danger, but he also loved me enough to respect what I had to do.

And then we chose names. In the end it was actually very easy. Mac's late parents had meant the world to him and they had very beautiful names.

"Everyone, I'd like to introduce you to our children," I said as emotion welled up inside me. "This is Audrey Hildegard and this is Henry Charles."

Out of the corner of my eye, I saw Mac and his brother Jacob hug each other tight. It sent me over the edge and I cradled my babies close. I'd never had a sibling, but Mac did and our children had each other. As of right now, I was fairly certain I wasn't going to get knocked up ever, ever, ever again... but who new what the future held?

"The names are perfect," Baba Yaga announced grandly. "And the Goddess sends her love. Audrey Hildegard and Henry Charles are very special people. There are no others in existence like them. I charge everyone in this room to watch over them and keep them safe. They will play very important roles in the future."

"Would you like to be a bit more specific?" I asked her with narrowed eyes.

"Of course not, darling! Where would the fun be in that?"

As Sassy and Jeeves passed around the food, I noticed Baba Yaga and Marge in deep conversation. Baba pointed to Sassy and Marge squealed with joy. Marge's eyes stayed glued on Sassy for the rest of the gathering.

Holy hell on a broom, if that conversation was what I thought it was, Sassy and Marge were in for some hellacious times together in the very near future. Thankfully if Sassy was Marge's *replacement*, it was not my problem. Who was I kidding? Sassy was always going to be my problem. I rolled my eyes to the ceiling when I realized I wanted it that way.

As for Bermangoogleshitz... I would tell Sassy about him when the time was right. But that wasn't today. Today was a day for celebration. And that's exactly what I was going to do.

Bob the beaver was the official baby photographer and took enough pictures of the glorious day to fill many albums. My obese cats left briefly and came back with two tiny kittens. They were the familiars in training for Audrey and Henry.

"We's gonna train them fuzzy little shits good," Fat Bastard promised as the mewing kittens settled themselves right next to Henry and Audrey.

"And we's not gonna give them no spray paint," Jango assured me.

"Well, not untils they're a little older," Boba Fett added much to Mac's displeasure.

I laughed and listened to the kittens purr with contentment next to their new charges. Then my eyes grew wide and my smile even wider.

"Can I name them?" I asked my three rotund furry nightmares.

"Sure youse can," Fat Bastard told me.

Glancing at the little kittens, I knew without a doubt that I'd chosen the ideal names. "Their names are Lucky and Charm," I stated with a giggle.

Mac's laugh went all through me and my tiny babies cooed their approval. The homage to my favorite cereal didn't work for my children, but was outstandingly well suited for their cats.

"The monikers are very fitting," Baba Yaga said with her hand tucked firmly and lovingly into my father's.

She was correct.

Life was good.

We were very lucky and most certainly charmed.

The End... For Now

Want more? A current list of my books is included at the end of this book.

KEEP READING in this book for bonus excerpts from authors Ann Charles and Donna McDonald.

Note From the Author

If you enjoyed this book, please consider leaving a positive review or rating on the site where you purchased it. Reader reviews help my books continue to be valued by resellers and help new readers make decisions about reading them. You are the reason I write these stories and I sincerely appreciate each of you!

Many thanks for your support,
~ Robyn Peterman

Visit my website at **www.robynpeterman.com** for more information about this series.

Want to hear about my new releases?
Sign-up for my newsletter.

Excerpt from
Nearly Departed In Deadwood

Book 1 of the
DEADWOOD HUMOROUS MYSTERY SERIES

By
Ann Charles

Book Description

"The first time I came to Deadwood, I got shot in the ass."--
Violet Parker

Little girls are vanishing from Deadwood, South Dakota, and Violet Parker's daughter could be next. She's desperate to find the monster behind the abductions. But if she's not careful, Violet just might end up as one of Deadwood's dearly departed.

Chapter 1

The first time I came to Deadwood, I got shot in the ass. Now, twenty-five years later, as I stared into the double barrels of Old Man Harvey's shotgun, irony was having a fiesta and I was the piñata.

I tried to produce a polite smile, but my cheeks had petrified along with my heart. "You wouldn't shoot a girl, would you?"

Old Man Harvey snorted, his whole face contorting with the effort. "Lady, I'd blow the damned Easter bunny's head off if he was tryin' to take what's mine."

He cocked his shotgun—his version of an exclamation mark.

"Whoa!" I would have gulped had there been any spit left in my mouth. "I'm not here to take anything."

He replied by aiming those two barrels at my chest instead of my face.

"I'm with Calamity Jane Realty, I swear! I came to ..."

With Harvey threatening to fill my lungs with peepholes, I had trouble remembering why I'd driven out to this corner of the boonies. Oh, yeah. Lowering one of my hands, I held out my crushed business card. "I want to help you sell your ranch."

The double barrels clinked against one of the buttons on my Rebecca Taylor-knockoff jacket as Harvey grabbed my card. I swallowed a squawk of panic and willed the soles of my boots to unglue from the floorboards of Harvey's front porch and retreat. Unfortunately, my brain's direct line to my feet was experiencing technical difficulties.

Harvey's squint relaxed. "Violet Parker, huh?"

"That's me." My voice sounded pip-squeaky in my own ears. I couldn't help it. Guns made my thighs wobbly and my bladder heavy. Had I not made a pit stop at Girdy's Grill for a buffalo burger and paid a visit to the little *Hens* room, I'd have a puddle in the bottom of my favorite cowboy boots by now.

"Your boots match your name. What's a 'Broker Associate'?"

"It's someone who is going to lose her job if she doesn't sell a house in the next three weeks." I lowered my other hand.

I'd been with Calamity Jane Realty for a little over two months and had yet to make a single sale. So much for my radical, life-changing leap into a new career. If I didn't make a sale before my probation was up, I'd have to drag my kids back down to the prairie and bunk with my parents ... again.

"You're a lot *purtier* in this here picture with your hair down."

"So I've been told." Old Man Harvey seemed to be channeling my nine-year-old daughter today. Lucky me.

"Makes you look younger, like a fine heifer."

I cocked my head to the side, unsure if I'd just been tossed a compliment or slapped with an insult.

The shotgun dipped to my belly button as he held the card out for me to take back.

"Keep it. I have plenty." A whole box full. They helped fill the lone drawer in my desk back at Calamity Jane's.

"So that asshole from the bank didn't send you?"

"No." An asshole from my office had, and the bastard would be extracting his balls from his esophagus for this so-called *generous referral*—if I made it back to Calamity Jane's without looking like a human sieve.

"Then how'd you know about my gambling problem?"

"What gambling problem?"

Old Man Harvey's eyes narrowed again. He whipped the double barrels back up to my kisser. "The only way you'd know I'm thinking about selling is if you heard about my gambling debt."

"Oh, you mean *that* gambling problem."

"What'd you think I meant?"

Bluffing was easier when I wasn't chatting up a shotgun. "I thought you were referring to the ... um ..." A tidbit of a phone conversation I'd overheard earlier this morning came to mind. "To the problem you had at the Prairie Dog Palace."

Harvey's jaw jutted. "Mud wrestling has no age limit."

"You're right. They need to be less age-biased. Maybe even have an *AARP Night* every Wednesday."

"Nobody told me about the bikini bit 'til it was too late."

I winced. I couldn't help it.

"So, what're you gonna charge me to sell my place?"

"What would you like me to charge you?" I was all about pleasing the customer this afternoon.

He leaned the gun on his shoulder, double barrels pointed at the porch ceiling. "The usual, I guess."

No longer on the verge of extinction, I used the porch rail to keep from keeling over. Maybe I just wasn't cut out for the realty business. Did they still sell encyclopedias door-to-door?

"This ranch belonged to my pappy, and his pappy before him." Harvey's lips thinned as he stared over my shoulder.

"It must hold a big place in your heart." I tried to sound sincere as I inched along the railing toward the steps. My red Bronco glinted and beckoned under the July sun.

"Hell, no. I can't wait to shuck this shithole."

"What?" I'd made it as far as the first step.

"I'm sick and tired of fixin' rusted fences, chasing four-wheeling fools through my pastures, sniffing out lost cows in every damned gulch and gully." His blue eyes snapped back to mine. "And I keep hearing funny noises at night coming from out behind my ol' barn."

I followed the nudge of his bearded chin. Weathered and white-washed by Mother Nature, the sprawling building's roof seemed to sag in the afternoon heat. The doors were chained shut, one of the haymow windows broken. "Funny how?"

"Like grab-your-shotgun funny."

Normally, this might give me pause, but after the greeting I'd received today from the old codger's double barrels, I had a feeling that Harvey wore his shotgun around the house like a pair of holey underwear. I'd bet my measly savings he even slept with it. "Maybe it's just a mountain lion," I suggested. "The paper said there's been a surge of sightings lately."

"Maybe. Maybe not," Harvey shrugged. "I don't care. I want to move to town. It gets awful lonely out here come wintertime. Start thinking about things that just ain't right. I almost married a girl from Taiwan last January. Turned out 'she' was really a 'he' from Nigeria."

"Wow."

"Damned Internet." Harvey's gaze washed over me. "What about you, Violet Parker?"

"What about me?"

"There's no ring on your finger. You got a boyfriend?"

"Uh, no."

I didn't want one, either. Men had a history of fouling up my life, from burning down my house to leaving me knocked up with twins. These days, I liked my relationships how I liked my eggs: over-easy.

Harvey's two gold teeth twinkled at me through his whiskers. "Then how about a drink? Scotch or gin?"

I chewed on my lip, considering my options. I could climb into my Bronco and watch this opportunity and the crazy old bastard with the trigger-happy finger disappear in my rearview mirror; or I could blow off common sense and follow Harvey in for some hard liquor and maybe a signed contract.

Like I really had a choice. "Do you have any tonic?"

Excerpt from
How To Train A Witch

Book 1 of the BABA YAGA SAGA

By

Donna McDonald

Book Description

To Baba Yaga or not to Baba Yaga? THAT was the big question.

Too bad no one knew the answer. Carol and Hildy were being tested, but evidently so was she. She was still the Jezibaba, yet all she could do was watch and worry while two people she deeply cared about went to meet their fate. What if that fate meant fighting demons? What would happen to all of them if the Chosen Ones failed? Morgana was threatening to make her immortal. That was definitely not a good sign.

As if the whole Baba Yaga thing wasn't trouble enough, she kept tripping over a wicked fairy Morgana made her set free. The situation set her instincts singing, but she had no one to talk to about it. She and Damien were still together—sort of—but the emotional distance between them had worsened over the years.

There was no time to learn meditation, but she still had to somehow find a place of calm. Until she officially retired the Jezibaba position, she couldn't take on any additional challenges. Her current chaos was enough to send any stressed witch on a no holds barred zapping spree.

Chapter 1

Making a quiet, sedate entrance had never been her style, but getting struck by lightning would definitely be a mood buster. Winds of change were blowing all around.

The edges of her red dress fluttered around her legs as the seven of them materialized on the lawn of the Witchery U campus. Jezibaba looked up at the rumbling sky and read the darkening clouds before sighing at the violent storm she felt brewing. She told herself the lack of welcoming sunshine didn't matter. It wasn't necessarily a bad omen.

But then it wasn't just the weather she was questioning.

Looking across the manicured campus lawn, she watched a bunch of teenagers playing some sort of game. The boys pelted each other with balls thrown from skinny stick baskets. The girls cheered and yelled at the boys. She rolled her eyes at the nonsense of it, even though they appeared to be having a good time.

Thank the Goddess those years were several centuries behind her. She cringed just thinking about all the emotional drama the very young delighted in putting themselves through.

Yes, it was good to be older. It was even better to be an older witch whose power had yet to stop growing. Not that she wanted to keep the title of the great and powerful Jezibaba forever. Wasn't that why she was here? She had to find a way to keep her two replacements alive long enough to secede her.

"Gentlemen, I need to find the proper motivation for this task. Tell me again why our presence here is necessary. I'm not used to jobs where I don't have to kill someone."

Jezibaba rolled her eyes when she heard a shuffling of seven gray robes sweeping the grass behind her as they silently communicated with each other. They were probably drawing mental straws about who would give her the bad news.

All were male witches, or warlocks as her testosterone laden posse preferred to be called. They were powerful seers, great conjurers, and fairly good at fetching coffee. Outside of that though, they were merely a bunch of devout magicals stuck in their heads. In her opinion, the whole lot was afraid to use their damn balls.

No wonder the Jezibaba was always a female witch. A female's irrational anger fueled a what-the-hell bravery few males could ever match. Feeling it now, she pushed her long mass of curly red hair over both her shoulders as she turned to favor them with a knowing and superior smirk. Maybe glaring was a tad mean, but it felt so damn good to vent her frustration.

"Look, I'm not going to turn you guys into toads just for answering my question. I'm not in the mood to torture you today. It's just that I'm having trouble believing we have to be directly involved with the lives of two children. For Goddess's sake, Nathaniel—will you stop shuffling in your robe and *speak to me*. Why in Morgana's name are we here? Nothing seems amiss."

173

Her most trusted warlock finally cleared his throat. She had been with Nathaniel for two of her three centuries in service to the Council of Witches. The warlock looked older than dirt, but he was still her junior by nearly a hundred and fifty years. She trusted the man for many reasons, but she liked him because he was the only one of her warlocks who wasn't scared completely shitless of her.

And okay—maybe she liked the way Nathaniel talked to her. The man spoke like they were all still living in medieval times. Goddess knew, sometimes she wished they were, except for the whole lack of plumbing thing, of course.

"M'lady, the last divination of the Council of Witches revealed that the magical world would be switching to a multiple Baba Yaga system instead of continuing the current Jezibaba system of one witch protectoress. Two candidates have been deemed worthy prospects already. We're just here to check on them. Their identity is being kept as quiet as possible by Council order."

Jezibaba snorted over the last comment because she knew better. Her gaze went back to the cheering, squealing, annoying teenagers again.

"If the Council of Witches could be trusted to keep their silence on the matter, none of us would be here to check on the chosen ones. Personally, I trust your instincts about them being in danger far more than I trust the meager integrity of the Council. You all know how I feel about those backstabbing, sanctimonious, magic-wielding ass monkeys."

Ignoring the in-drawn breaths over her irreverent cursing, Jezibaba checked her nail polish before glancing at the teenagers again. She was not good at dealing with magical children of any age. The young tended to abuse their powers and that always made her angry. Her patience about such things was nil.

Nothing Nathaniel had said meant she had to oversee the brats personally. She would gladly find them guardians which was being far kinder than the previous Jezibaba had been to her. She'd almost been killed dozens of time before she hit her mid-twenties. In fact, she'd been a woman of twenty-six before she'd even begun her training.

"So the prophecy was correct then, I am to be the last of my kind unless I become a babysitter. Is that what you're telling me, Nathaniel?"

Her chief warlock stiffened behind her and his instant alertness to her tone made her smile.

"I'm not telling you to do anything, Jezibaba. I would never presume to do that. I am merely informing you of the same details we discussed yesterday when we were planning this trip. You alone will have to determine if the children need additional protection."

"I guess I'd pushed that annoying discussion from my mind."

She wanted to laugh when Nathaniel's eyes narrowed beneath his black hood.

"Don't get your loin cloth in a twist over my honesty. I'm here, aren't I?" she declared, lifting a hand to point to the teenagers.

Real intimidation was a power rush for her… and the closest thing to an orgasm she'd had in months. Men who could handle her real nature—and her power—didn't grow on trees, not even those in the sacred grove of Morgana The Red. She knew that for a fact because over the years, she'd bedded every mythical creature the Goddess had made, but had never found one she could care about more than a few months.

175

In the last decade, she'd shrunk to an all time low, seeking out those like herself who at least respected her magic. Unfortunately, she'd found nothing but self-absorbed warlocks who couldn't get a witch off properly without magical help. Her feminine ego had nearly hit rock bottom before she'd figured out that she was better off alone.

Maybe her libido was more unhappy over her abstinence than she'd realized because it suddenly conjured a man who gave her body hope. She lifted an eyebrow as she watched a professor exit one of the buildings and head towards another. Professor Hottie certainly filled out his clothes well for an intellectual type. Muscles rippled under the loose white shirt he wore beneath his forest green academic robe. His slacks molded the rest of his shape in a way that immediately jumpstarted a fantasy or two about what remained tantalizingly out of sight.

But something about him triggered a memory… or an instinct… or some sort of something. It was one of those feelings a smart witch would never ignore.

Dreading the truth but having to know, Jezibaba waved a hand over her eyes and swore at what her magical sight revealed. Knowing now what he truly was only made her appreciate her innate caution more. Professor Hottie, with all those rippling muscles, was a fire-breathing dragon, which meant he was totally off limits to her.

Sighing in resignation, Jezibaba gave up watching his sexy, masculine walk and started trudging towards the field of teens who were still screaming at each other. They had never ceased as far she could tell. Might as well get the introductions over with so she could put the frustrating day behind her as quickly as possible.

"Forgive me, m'lady… but you're going the wrong way."

Jezibaba swung a questioning gaze back to an equally confused Nathaniel, her eyebrows shooting up and making her whole facial expression match.

"What do you mean the wrong way?"

Nathaniel cleared his throat, adjusted his druidic style hood, and pointed a long boney finger at the building the now off-limits Professor Hottie had exited a few moments before.

Jezibaba fisted hands on her hips. "You can't be serious, Nathaniel. That's elementary level. Are you telling me the chosen ones are not even riding their brooms yet?"

Nathaniel nodded. "Believe me, mistress. I'm not confident in the matter either, but I consulted the Fates to check the Council's determinations."

"The Fates! Goddess, I hate those nosey old biddies." Jezibaba stalked back to the front with the rest of her warlock posse.

"Yes. Well, the feeling is mutual between you, M'lady. They seem to hate you as well."

Since killing Nathaniel was out of the question, Jezibaba genuinely glared at the messenger instead. "The Fates have a burr up their butts because I refuse to die on their command. If they don't like me surviving their many predictions, they can take it up with Morgana. She's the one who made me Jezibaba. I didn't have any choice in that either. It was decided generations before I was born."

"Regardless of your tragic history, I must unfortunately report that the two chosen ones are merely ten years old. I sought the counsel of the Fates in order to confirm their ages. The Fates laughed when I asked for more information. They said we'd have no trouble finding them if we went looking. Both descend from proper lineages. There's no other reason to question this, unless you can think of some reason the other warlocks and I haven't."

Jezibaba sighed in frustration. "No. I guess I can't think of any reason the chosen ones can't be ten if they're freaking ten. Very well, Nathaniel. What are their names?"

"Hildy and Carol."

"Rather ordinary names for the chosen ones," Jezibaba said, making a face.

"Indeed, M'lady. I thought the same. Your birth given name is much nicer," Nathaniel stated.

"Oh, you're sucking up now? Good show, Nathaniel. That's why you're still my favorite."

With a long suffering sigh, Jezibaba started towards the "right" building, her fashionable red dress billowing in the breeze. The first thing she'd done when she'd inherited the position was change the damn dress code. She was the Jezibaba—the most powerful witch ever born—not some drab mythological hag from a children's story.

She refused to wear her ceremonial black robe for anything but Council proceedings. She wanted to garner attention, not pity, from those who saw her. The red dress was far more striking and commanded a lot more attention when she needed to get people focused on doing her will. Nathaniel carried both her emergency witch hat and her ceremonial robe within his own grim looking clothes. That was as traditional as she was freaking willing to be.

Before she could put out a hand, the youngest of the warlock posse scrambled around her to open the door. She had barely nodded at his deference when Professor Hottie zoomed through the opening ahead of her, cutting her entry off on his mad dash inside. Her indignant huff over his rudeness caught his attention. Instead of apologizing though, he turned to her and smiled.

"Sorry, beautiful. You have very nice legs, but I'm extremely late for class," he explained, his admiring gaze dropping to them as he spoke.

Jezibaba stepped through the door enough to allow Nathaniel to enter behind her. "How would you like to teach class as a giant dragon toad today?" she asked faux politely.

Even knowing the fire-breather was on her forbidden list, Professor Hottie's husky chuckle over her threat still made her woo-hoo vibrate. She raised a hand to make good on her threat—and to show her woo-hoo who was boss—but lowered it when two children rushed out of a nearby classroom and grabbed one long, incredible fit man's leg each.

The Council of Witches would fine her and reduce her salary if she reduced innocent kids to tadpoles for no good reason. Goddess knew, she couldn't afford any garnishments. Retirement was on the horizon for her and she was hording every cent she made. Her daily ritual of checking her investments allowed her to sleep more peacefully at night.

"Professor Smoke, did you see them run out here?" Hildy demanded.

"See who, Hildy?" he asked gently, running a hand over her hair.

"The kittens. They were three of the tiniest, cutest kittens ever. They danced and let me pet them before they disappeared."

"Because *I* scared them away," Carol bragged, laughing as she looked up in her favorite teacher's face. "But I swear I didn't hurt them, Professor Smoke. I just let them blink out the way they wanted. I even waved goodbye and they said they'd see me again."

"*Us* again—they said they would see *us* again," Hildy corrected.

"No. *Me*," Carol insisted. "They said *me*. You just can't believe animals might like me better than you for once. Admit it, Hildy."

"How would you like to look like the big lying toad you are, Carol?" Hildy demanded. She turned loose and raised her hands.

Jezibaba fought back a grin when Professor Hottie's larger ones closed around the little witch's hands while he shook his head in warning.

"Hildy, do you want to lose your recess privileges and your best friend?"

Jezibaba covered her mouth as Carol turned loose of his leg, crossed her arms, and smirked when Hildy narrowed her eyes.

"They said *me*, Hildy. Live with it."

To keep from openly laughing—and from being pissed at the Fates for being right about these two miscreants—Jezibaba decided she needed to intervene. She let loose a shrill whistle which split the air, effectively ending the debate. All eyes turned to her with proper respect at last as she slowly removed her fingers from her teeth.

Professor Hottie had the audacity to wink at her attention-getting ploy. She gave him a warning finger wag for his grin which she took as flirting because his gaze kept returning to her legs. The girls were both still frozen in place, staring at her in outright fear now, which suited her just fine. But she ignored them to glance over her shoulder and smirk at the cloaked warlock staring at them in equal shock.

"The future's so damn bright, I need to wear shades… or maybe have ten tankards of troll ale so I can deal with this," Jezibaba declared merrily, sweeping her hand at the frightened girls as she looked back at them. She snorted at their continued stares. "I swear if you two were older, I'd throw you both in the magic pokey and hire smelly tutors for you. I bet you'd learn to appreciate each other then."

Both girls drew in sharp breaths over the cursing… and the threat.

180

Jezibaba smiled brilliantly at their quaking knees, her power swelling to fill the area with a fine golden mist. Stressful situations caused the occasional power leak, but it was not enough to worry her. No one seemed to mind walking around in gold glitter when it happened and she'd always liked sparkly things anyway.

"M'lady—it's impossible not to notice that the one named Hildy apparently shares your fondness for turning people into amphibians," Nathaniel pointed out, leaning in close enough to her to whisper. "However, Carol's superior attitude is oddly reminiscent of your demeanor when we first met. They are both tiny mirrors of your greatness."

"They're children, Nathaniel. Just children," Jezibaba declared, but she could also feel their power tugging on hers as they stared. "Neither can be called yet and I won't allow it to happen anyway. The Council is probably just worried because I've served longer than any Jezibaba before me. I realize three hundred and sixty-six seems old to some of them, but I don't look a day over a human fifty. And these children are not—I repeat *not*—to be called until they are of a proper age to choose the path for themselves."

Professor Hottie held her gaze as he leaned down to talk to his charges. "Girls, head to class now. Tell Ms Turner to start reading the spells, but no casting until I get there."

When they didn't move, Jezibaba met his inquisitive gaze and shrugged to show him she was not holding them with any kind of restraining spell.

Grinning at her reaction, he lifted the girls by the backs of their shirts and turned them away from her. Once released from his hold, they shot off into the room like bolts of lightning flying off his fingertips.

Jezibaba watched Professor Hottie turn and walk slowly toward her. His guard was up now, wondering who and what she really was. But she could tell his worry was mostly for the children and rightly so. They would need a champion or two... or seventy... before they were old enough and strong enough to take over her work.

When Professor Hottie stopped, her heart fluttered in response to the dragon's protective stance. Goddess, it would have been nice to have had someone like him guarding her while she was growing up. It might even be nice to have someone like that having her back now.

One of the advantages of being older was that she knew better than to take her attraction to the dragon shifter seriously. She wouldn't call it being wiser exactly. More like street smart and maybe she was simply not stupid enough to fall too hard for a nice ass anymore. Most nice asses had a matching one sitting on their shoulders. She'd learned that the hard way, as she had every other hard lesson.

Bottom line for her flutters? Her insides needed to stop that shit. No way was she letting a dragon into her pants just because he cared for her future replacements. No witch with any sense would stoop so low. Even if dragons hadn't been on her don't-fuck list, they had a tendency to mark females they slept with so no other dragon would go there. She was not getting a dragon fire created v-jay-jay tattoo guaranteed to wilt the dick of any future lover she took.

Her attention left her thoughts and returned to him when she realized he was scanning her face and not her legs anymore.

"You're the Jezibaba. I'm sorry I didn't recognize you. I'm Professor Damien Smoke."

A sharp retort about his oversight was on her tongue. It hovered there letting her taste the pleasure it would give her to say it and see his eyes flash in anger. But the nastiness just wouldn't come out. Damn her weakness for sexy men.

"Quite understandable given the circumstances, Professor. Your primary focus wasn't on me," she answered calmly.

"No, but we both know my attention could be on you if you wanted it to be," Damien replied smoothly, grinning when her eyebrows shot up again. "Sorry. I can't seem to behave any better than the girls today. It's just that you're every bit as mesmerizing in person as I imagined you being. Of course you were alluring even before when I thought you were just... never mind that. Perhaps I better shut up now."

Pretending not to care was a trick to pull off, but she'd had a lot of practice doing so in her life. "No worries, Professor. Power. Glamour. It momentarily draws attention. You'll forget me a few minutes after the warlocks and I leave. In my experience, most unnatural enchantments never last longer than that, though I promise you, I do nothing to draw it on purpose. It is innate."

Professor Hottie looked thoughtful for a moment, opened his mouth to speak, but then appeared to change his mind. When her stomach dropped in disappointment, Jezibaba narrowed her eyes.

"I came here on business. Point me to your headmaster," she ordered, wanting to move things along. Action would no doubt lessen the distraction Professor Hottie presented.

Chuckling, Professor Hottie reached out and lifted one of her hands before she could stop him. Magic buzzed along her palm and down to her fingertips. He kissed the back of her hand reverently as was due someone in her position, and then shocked her by placing her palm flat on his well-endowed chest. The contact was just as nice as she'd expected it might be.

"The unfortunate headmaster of Witchery U stands before you—guilty as charged. I'm the one you seek, but you can call me Damien."

Jezibaba slid her hand away, remembering the heat of his muscles even after the contact was broken. Damn dragon. Damn sexy, panty-melting dragon. He'd made her touch him on purpose. Why was he being so charming? He was hiding something—trying to distract her further. That had to be the case. Well, it wouldn't work. She'd dealt with sneaky dragons before.

In fact, there wasn't much she hadn't dealt with in her tenure as the current witch protectoress. Professor Hottie might be teaching the future versions of her—and lucky them for it—but she had been taught at the school of hard knock spells, troll curses, and angry gods with vendettas.

"I've come about two of your students, Professor. Apparently, they've been chosen as my potential replacements," she stated stiffly. "We're not taking them today of course."

She turned around to the grumbling warlocks behind her who had quietly filed inside the building behind Nathaniel. "No, we are absolutely not taking them. They're children. Did you hear me? *Children.*"

She turned back to the sexy dragon and smiled as neutrally as possible. "We just wanted to make you aware of their futures, Professor Smoke. Perhaps recommend you take a few extra precautions with their safety."

"You're talking about Hildy and Carol," Damien stated.

"Yes," Jezibaba confirmed. "I am speaking of Hildy and Carol."

He nodded as he thought about it. "I knew those two were powerful. We always look out for those with that level of magic at their beckoning—mostly because they be a danger to everyone—but they're only ten. Real power doesn't manifest at such a young age. I find it hard to believe they've been singled out already."

Jezibaba nodded and frowned. "Indeed. You echo my concerns, Professor Smoke. This early tapping of my prospective replacements is a strange situation. I'm sure in a couple of decades their power will make it obvious they should be considered contenders. Though it's not unheard of to be singled out early. In fact, I was chosen before I was born. When I got my menses, I fully expected the warlocks to come get me, but they never... *what now*?"

Jezibaba stopped her story and shook her head at the rumbling and groaning going on behind her. Her gaze met the sexy dragon's. "I could write a damn book about the fragile sensibilities of warlocks. They don't like to think about the fact I'm female in all regards."

Professor Hottie's responding grin made her day. It was nice to finally have someone recognize the political agony she bore for the sake of doing her job.

"So you were chosen shortly after your passage into womanhood?" he prompted.

She snorted at his words. "More like I was expecting someone to come collect me. Passage into womanhood? You're obviously much better with nice words than I am. Not surprising, given your profession, I suppose."

"On the contrary, you might be more surprised by my past than you ever imagined. I wasn't always a teacher. Perhaps we can have dinner sometime and share our stories. I would like that very much. But for now, let me tell Ms Turner to finish the lesson. We can go to my office and talk about what measures need to be taken for the children's safety. Have their parents been told about the prophecy?"

"No," Jezibaba said firmly. "And we have no intentions of telling them until it is unavoidable. There is enough drama happening. The Council of Witches and the Fates have chosen my successors, but I will choose their protectors. There is discord in both of the children's families and no one is going to take their normal life from them a moment sooner than necessary if I can prevent it from happening. That is my firm decision about the matter."

Her eyes blazed with determination and only softened when Professor Hottie bowed to her.

"I agree with you and it will be my pleasure to see your will about this manifest," he promised. "Now excuse me for a moment and I will join you in my office."

Charmed despite her misgivings, she fought off her urge to sigh in frustration. "Why did you have to be a damn dragon?" she whispered under her breath.

For a second time that day, she couldn't stop herself from staring at Professor Damien Smoke's perfect ass as he disappeared into the classroom.

Chapter 2

Always on guard, Nathaniel stared out of the room's single window, while she stared at Professor Hottie. She was finding it very challenging to have a conversation about something other than the two of them running off alone.

No matter how much her inner witch chanted "no dragon, no dragon". All she really wanted was to curl up in his lap and wriggle until his control snapped and he threw her across his shiny, neat desk, and... *damn it.*

Jezibaba sat up straighter in the chair, but it was hard shaking off her fantasy. It had been a long time since simple lust had taken her mind off her business so completely. Now she'd missed what Professor Hottie had said while she was imagining him naked on top of her.

Her frustrated groan garnered both Nathaniel's and Professor Hottie's full attention. Hellcat's fury. Her sexual deprivation didn't matter. Protecting her successors did.

"Are children their age allowed their familiars yet?"

Professor Hottie frowned at her question. Even that was hot. Dragon hot... but still... hot. She ran both hands through her hair and reminded herself of her purpose. Professor Hottie glanced behind him to study Nathaniel standing like a sentinel. The warlock's attention seemed fixed on the manicured campus lawn, but she knew he was listening to every word that was said.

"Speak your mind freely, Professor Smoke. I trust Nathaniel with my life and do so every day. All day. He came with the job and yes... I had no say in the matter. However, he's the only one of the warlock posse I bring into serious discussions like this. Now speak. I'm getting edgy and impatient."

"Yes. I can tell. You get all glittery when you get tense."

Jezibaba snorted when Professor Hottie's gaze fell to her ample cleavage before rising back to her eyes. It sent her off into another fantasy. She pulled her mind back with a hiss. "I'm still waiting, Professor..."

"At the risk of offending you, I don't think you heard what I said just now. The girls have been attacked twice already. One attack was a swarm of insects which they took care of themselves without even understanding the danger."

"And the second attack?"

"It happened just a few hours ago and I had to incinerate a vampire assassin disguised as a giant bat. The girls thought I had killed a real bat. When you arrived, I was taking his ashes to the high school science lab to see if they could find out who sent him."

188

"But we just found out about the girls two days ago…" Jezibaba stopped her defense. It was useless. There was only one real explanation for the attacks. "Someone on the Council must be trying to kill them. Whoever it is wants to end the cycle. Without a witch protectoress, the Council of Witches's combined power would rule the magical world. I can't let that happen, Professor Smoke. No Council will protect the magical community as me and my predecessors have done—not to mention what could happen to all the humans in our lives."

She leaned back in her chair. Nathaniel's gaze turned to her. He was thoughtful for a moment and then nodded in agreement with her rant. She swore internally. Damn. There went her easing into retirement plans while she pretended to babysit.

She nodded back that she accepted his judgment in the matter. The truth did not make her happy—not at all. Now she had no choice but to get involved.

Professor Smoke put an elbow on his desk and leaned forward. "After the insects, I called up my horde and got some of my old guards to come watch over the girls. Dragon warriors are pretending to be janitors, teachers, assistants, and the younger ones are college placed student aides. What they don't have to pretend is how deadly they are, especially since they'd be immune to shifters and vamps. Whoever is after the girls is in for a big surprise the next time they try something."

Jezibaba stood because she needed to pace. It helped her think. Nathaniel's eyebrows rose when she put her hands behind her back. He knew it meant she didn't trust her hands not to conjure up something to match her darkening mood. The idea of the children being targets went way beyond them being her replacements. They must be truly powerful… which meant they had to be protected until they came into full use of their magic.

She stopped and glared across the room. "Is this why you wanted to take the children and lock them away? You knew they were in trouble, Nathaniel?"

Nathaniel shook his head. "No. Only suspected, M'lady. Being in danger was merely conjecture on my part without any evidence to back it up."

"*Conjecture?* You're the most proficient seer who's ever lived," Jezibaba declared sharply. "And we've already had this ageist discussion. You and I might be waning in some ways, but trust your magic, old friend. Use every ounce up until it's really gone. Don't let self-doubt rob you of a single second."

She frowned and shook her head when Nathaniel turned back to the window without answering. She hadn't meant to lecture him in front of an audience. It had just slipped out.

Worry made her tongue sharp and her brain irrational. That hadn't changed for her in over three hundred years. She'd just learned to work around it. But even her Goddess had given up trying to tame her bossiness.

She would have to do something to apologize to Nathaniel later. Making personal amends when she was wrong was more of a challenge than killing a thousand evil magicals.

Mind returning to the task at hand, she felt Professor Hottie's gaze on her again and turned to meet it. "With death threats happening, I can't avoid being involved in all plans for their safety. I want the girls to have their familiars. It is my intention to talk you into this, Professor Smoke. How hard is it going to be?"

His lips twisted into a sexy grimace as he considered it. She'd love nothing more than to bite that lip he was punishing with his very sharp-looking teeth. She'd crawl into his lap, plant her ass over his rising... shitballs. What was wrong with her freaking mind today? Lust never did this to her—never.

"The other children are not going to like the situation," Damien warned.

Jezibaba shrugged. "Tell them Hildy and Carol earned their familiars because of their progress. We'll let one or two other exemplary students have them as well. That should lay rumors to rest and give them all a goal worth striving for. This is only a year or two earlier than it is usually done. I will take care of the bestowance."

Professor Hottie's beaming smile had her hand coming to her stomach to calm the flutters it evoked in her. She had a feeling she could chant "no dragon" all day long and it would never lessen the power that flash of white teeth would have over her.

"Jezibaba—I think you'd make a damn good teacher," he said sincerely.

At the praise, she favored him with a beaming smile herself. He leaned forward on his desk, his own smile fading. She knew it was to hide what was happening in his lap and she enjoyed the feeling of getting a little even with him. The wickedness conveyed in her twinkling gaze affected every male she encountered to some degree, but she was thrilled to know Professor Hottie—the off-limits dragon—wasn't immune to her.

"I'm so glad you think that, Professor Smoke. Because there's a second part to my plan."

***

191

Damien couldn't keep the smile from his face as he introduced her. All eyes were glued to the mesmerizing witch at his side and he hadn't had to chastise a single student to get their complete attention focused up front.

"Class, this is the Jezibaba. I'm sure you've heard your parents talking about her. She's started a new education project here at Witchery U and will be one of your teachers for the rest of this academic year. One of her many specialties is magical protection, so you'll be learning all sorts of ways to protect yourselves in her classes."

A student raised their hand. Damien sighed and nodded. "Yes, Rory?"

Rory squirmed in his chair, but finally mustered up his courage. "My dad said the Jezibaba turns people into toads when she gets mad at them. Is she allowed to turn us into toads if we're bad, Professor Smoke?"

"What's so scary about that, Rory? Hildy does that too when she gets mad at us," Carol blurted out. "It just doesn't last long because she's a magical wimp."

"I am not a wimp," Hildy declared. "I just don't want to hurt people. All I try to do is stop them from making me angrier."

Jezibaba narrowed her eyes at Carol who shrunk down in her seat under her stare. She turned a smile to the original questioner.

"That's a very good question, Rory. I suggest you don't make me angry enough to test the theory and get a personal answer. My spells last quite a bit longer than Hildy's—like hundreds of years longer."

Rory's eyes widened as he nodded. "Yes, ma'am. Jezibaba, ma'am."

Damien fought back a smile when Jezibaba's twinkling, amused gaze met his. She shrugged her elegant shoulders.

"I hope my honesty with your students doesn't offend you, Professor. I used to incarcerate magic abusers. But the jails got full and there was all that overhead to feed the prisoners. There's so much more room in nature. I find a few days catching flies and croaking as a toad work just as well as a few years spent behind bars," she explained.

He covered his mouth so the students wouldn't catch him smiling. He wiped it away before removing his hand, but it was difficult. "Your restraint in my classroom will be appreciated, Jezibaba. We don't have that many flies around campus," Damien said gravely.

Jezibaba turned and faced all the frightened stares. "Fear, such as you are feeling about me, is a healthy response. My power is great and yours is not. All strangers with magic require approaching with caution. I'm going to show you some tricks about how to protect yourselves, but today's not a day for those lessons. Today, four of you whose power has manifested greatly already will receive a first line personal protector. We are assigning familiars a bit earlier than usual."

Her gaze zeroed back to her questioner. She motioned with a hand. "Come forward, Rory. You're on my list."

Rory's eyes widened in alarm and his classmates drew in a breath as they turned to stare at him. Jezibaba enjoyed knowing he wanted to pee his pants, but that wasn't going to serve her purposes. She didn't want to spare the time the boy would need to change clothes.

"I promise not to turn you into a toad today. Witches Honor," Jezibaba said sharply. "Now come here. When a challenge is presented, a confident witch or warlock should never hesitate. In your hesitation, your adversary will have ample time to finish a spell. Disrupt their thinking in any manner possible as you challenge. Can you walk a little faster, boy? I'm aging as you dawdle."

Damien watched as Rory picked up his pace, but only barely. Finally, the kid stopped about two feet in front of her.

Jezibaba paced around him, turning her head. "Lift your chin," she ordered, and Rory complied. "Ah, you have a nice long neck. Are you afraid of snakes, Rory?"

"No ma'am—I mean—no Jezibaba ma'am."

"Good," she declared and pulled a two foot gold and black snake out of one of her sleeves.

When it hissed at her, she hissed back and spoke to it in a tongue Damien had never heard leave a woman's mouth. The witch was obviously well versed in reptilian languages. He found himself wondering if she spoke dragon.

Smiling she walked to Rory. "Hold out your arm, boy."

When he did, she placed the snake's head on his hand. The snake wound slowly around his arm, crawling until it had wrapped itself lightly around the boy's neck. The snake hissed, its tongue flicking against Rory's cheek making him giggle. He looked beyond delighted, which delighted her in return.

"After you trust him, get him to bite you. Then you two can share thoughts with each other. His name is Saigon. This is his normal form, but he has others. It costs him greatly to use his magic to shift to them, so he won't change forms until there is dire need. You must care for Saigon as you would yourself, Rory. He will protect you with his very life. Be worthy of the sacrifice or no other familiars will have anything to do with you in the future."

"Yes, ma'am—I mean, I will—Jezibaba ma'am. I like him. He's really cool."

"I know. Now take him back with you to your seat. He must stay with you at all times. You can wear him like a scarf, but sometimes he likes to sleep inside your clothes where it's warm. He'll most likely leave you at night to hunt, but he'll always return by morning."

Damien grinned when Rory looked up at Jezibaba in adoration, even as she turned him and gave him a shove to get him walking. He felt his giant dragon's heart squeeze alarmingly within his chest. The woman was a legendary badass. It made her huge efforts to shield these innocents from her true nature all the more impressive.

"Hildy. Come forward," she called, tucking her hands behind her back.

Braver now because of Rory, Hildy slid from her seat and walked to where she stood. Damien fought back a chuckle when the girl swallowed hard as Jezibaba looked down in her eyes.

"It is very difficult to choose a familiar for someone with your affinity for all Morgana's creatures, but we'll do the best we can. I believe I heard you asking Professor Smoke about some special kittens."

Hildy nodded. "Yes. They come, but they don't stay long. I see them all the time."

"I bet they are asking permission to be your familiars—all three. It is very rare to get a group like that. Only special witches get those sorts of followings," Jezibaba said sharply. "Have you asked them to stay with you?"

Damien snapped to attention when Jezibaba's gaze darkened. It went across the room to Carol shifting in her seat and frowning. He went on alert when she chastised the girl.

"The kittens are Hildy's. And they will see you again because you are Hildy's best friend. So there was no lying in their statements. Get that unworthy thought out of your head before it turns to a darkness you can't control. Am I being clear, Carol?"

Carol hung her head and nodded.

Jezibaba's gaze lightened as it came back to Hildy. "Now I wish your future could be different, but it cannot. Natural healers bear a great burden, but they also have a capacity to appreciate joy in a way most creatures don't. So you might as well have amusing familiars to keep your heart light and a smile on your face. Call them to you, child. Call them like you usually do."

Damien heard Carol snort, but she sunk into the seat when Jezibaba glared at her for the noise she made. He turned back as Hildy made a face.

"Here, kitty, kitty, kitty."

Jezibaba snorted. "Do they actually come for that weak calling? No. Try again, Hildy. Forget all of us. Call them as if we were not present in the room. Do it, girl."

Hildy frowned and stooped to the floor. She patted it three times, putting her concentration into her palm hitting the cool tile.

"Here. Kitty. Kitty. Kitty."

Three kittens appeared out of thin air, materializing within reach of her hands. She laughed as she petted them.

"Jezibaba said you can stay with me and be my familiars. I would like that. Please stay."

Damien's eyebrows rose when the kittens froze in place and turned their heads to stare at Jezibaba. He smelled large amounts of fear radiating off all three of them. She was glaring at the kittens, one eyebrow raised in question.

"Did you think I didn't know you keep sneaking out of your confinement? Your vile personal habits best not ever be a part of this child's life—and I mean ever—or you will all three spend the other seven of your lives living as toads instead of cats. Now promise to serve Hildy during this life you now lead. In exchange, I will lift the remainder of your punishment and restore your powers."

Damien stood transfixed as the kittens trotted over to the Jezibaba, wound themselves around her ankles one at a time, and then trotted back to Hildy and did the same to her.

"Good. It is done then," Jezibaba declared. "Hildy, you don't have to pat the ground anymore. They'll come for any call you make. Kittens are a little more distracting than a snake or a grown cat though during school hours. I would suggest you let them blink out and come to you only when you want them around."

Hildy's head bobbed fiercely. "Yes, Jezibaba. Thank you. They're wonderful. I will take the best of care of them."

"I know you will. You are welcome, child. Now say goodbye to them and return to your seat."

Hildy finger waved and said bye. She nearly skipped to her seat when the kittens disappeared. Her smile was radiant. It was the happiest Damien had ever seen her be.

Jezibaba called up a girl named Faith and gave her an older cat with one green eye and one blue. The cat trotted back to the seat with the girl and crawled under the desk to curl into a ball.

Then Jezibaba fisted her hands on her hips. "Carol—get up here. Don't dawdle. I need to be somewhere else shortly."

Looking anything but happy to be summoned so sternly, Carol trudged up to stand in front of Jezibaba lifting her chin and glaring back. Damien covered his mouth, this time to hide a grimace at the girl's show of disrespect. He was amazed when Jezibaba favored the girl with a wicked, beaming smile. To him, it was far more frightening, and Carol seemed to know it, but the kid was holding her own.

"Professor Smoke, please open the window. I need to call Carol's familiar to her," Jezibaba ordered.

She turned and smiled down at the girl as she gave a long suffering sigh.

"You like using your power against people. It makes you feel strong and I think you revel too much in that feeling. By the laws of the Goddess, I could lock you away for a hundred years even at your young age, but you'd just grow into a bitter martyr for evil. I can't allow that to happen to you because you're far too powerful a witch to not be serving the magical community."

Jezibaba wrestled her gaze away and walked in a circle around the child, chanting to constrain the girl from reacting when her familiar arrived. There was absolute silence in the room, but she could feel Hildy's worried gaze on them both. Jezibaba couldn't afford to comfort the other of her prospects, so she didn't bother to even glance her way. What was most important was that this mirror of her know she always meant exactly what she said.

"Carol, I'm assigning you a special guardian who will teach you right and wrong. He will judge your abuses, and if he finds you guilty, your familiar will mirror your spell back to you. Empathy is a very effective teaching tool. I can guarantee you will learn your lessons… just like I did under his tutelage. After you have sufficiently progressed in a few years, then you will be free to choose your own familiar. In the meantime, you will use *mine*."

Carol looked to the window in fear.

Jezibaba leaned down. "What kind of beast do you think my familiar is, child?" she whispered in her most stern voice, raising goosebumps on the girl's arms. "He is a powerful creature of many forms. Let's see what he chooses to show you first, shall we?"

Jezibaba stood tall and held out her arms. She put all the power she had into her voice, mostly for dramatic effect in this instance, but she knew her familiar would understand her reasons.

"Great Emeritus, come to me. As I will, so mote it be."

Damien winced as an ear shattering "Caw" filled the room as a giant black raven flew in the window and landed on Jezibaba's arm.

"I have a new pupil I would like you to consider," she said to the raven.

Damien saw the raven look down at Carol who stared up at him in great fear. The raven turned to Jezibaba and nodded his head, cawing again.

Then the bird lifted from her arm and transformed into a large black dog with hellhound teeth and red eyes. He landed lightly on the floor and paced around the girl, looking like he was going to eat her. Instead, the creature leaned in and licked the side of Carol's face with a large tongue.

"Oh, good. Emeritus has agreed to take you on," Jezibaba declared, clapping her hands once in great pleasure. "Now pet him. Go on. He's waiting for a sign of your agreement."

Carol looked at Jezibaba and back to the dog thing. "Do I have to pet him?"

"You were so brave earlier, Carol. Are you now afraid?" Jezibaba challenged.

"No," Carol protested, looking back at the waiting animal. She reached out a trembling hand and ran it down the dog's neck, shivering herself when it shivered under her touch. Whimpering, it turned to look at the Jezibaba.

"Yes, I know. I told you she was strong," Jezibaba said, speaking to the hellhound.

Damien watched the hellhound turn to look at Jezibaba, transforming once more, this time into a large white owl who jumped onto the edge of his lecturing podium.

Jezibaba bowed her head to the animal and went down to one knee. "Thank you, Great Emeritus. I do realize what I am asking, old friend. If Morgana favors me in my plans, this is the last pupil I will ask you to train."

Damien swallowed tightly at the sight they made. The Jezibaba never bowed to anyone—she didn't have to. The owl bobbed his head to her, then lifted into the air, becoming the giant black raven again before he flew back out of the window.

Jezibaba rose to her feet. She looked at Damien's shocked expression before moving to the girl's equally shocked one.

"A witch, no matter how powerful, is no match for a creature like Emeritus. He is a guardian of old and you should feel lucky he finds you worthy enough to serve, Child. You have been blessed this day in ways you will not understand until a hundred years from now. I hope you are good to him. Otherwise, Emeritus could bring about your death. He is a stronger believer in balance than I am."

Carol turned without prompting and returned to her seat. Damien saw her staring straight ahead. Jezibaba showed no remorse for terrifying the girl beyond anything he'd witnessed done to a student.

"Now I must go, but I will return soon. Professor—if you will show the warlocks to my room, they will see to it that my things are brought along. Until tomorrow…"

And just like that, she and Nathaniel were gone from the room. Damien looked around the class at the stunned faces. Their expressions probably mirrored his.

"Okay. Let's take a break. Pick a flying spell book from the bookshelves and we'll try it on one of the brooms later."

As the children scrambled, he walked to the window and closed it, sighing with relief that the school day was almost over, but also that Jezibaba said she was returning. She was the first female in the seventy-five years he'd been without a mate to stir in him an urge to seek a physical connection. Since he couldn't leave the school, it would be a lot easier to explore that strange urge she prompted if the powerful woman remained nearby.

And he certainly wasn't sure how he was going to explain to his pure dragon family he was falling for a witch, but he'd figure that one out once he knew if their connection held what their attraction promised.

Jezibaba or not, the witch was the first female he'd wanted in too long of a damn time. The magic of a dragon's desire for his female was far stronger than any spell a witch could ever weave. He'd been alone far too long. He would not risk turning away such a gift, even if the female had come into his life through the wicked Goddess, Morgana The Red.

Chapter 3

Jezibaba stood before her Goddess appointed employers and crossed her arms to keep from zapping all of them. Killing everyone on the existing Council of Witches would be one sure way of making sure the traitor was taken care of. Only the hassle of having to search for new politicians, rule makers, and money keepers kept her from it. She had faith that she would root out the weed eventually. It was the time required to do so that irritated her.

Their elected spokesman, an elderly neo-Druid, stood to address her. "Your time is far too valuable to be their guardian, Great One. What if something more important came up and you couldn't be reached?"

Jezibaba glared at him. "Nathaniel is blood bound to me. He can call me in an instant. I will always be able to be reached."

Before coming to see them, she'd covered her red dress with their butt ugly required black robe... and put on the stupid hat that made her look like some Medieval river dunking reject. The least they could do was listen to her full plan before refusing her outright. Not that the Council's opinions of her decisions were going to stop her. Her instincts were telling her she was right to be concerned.

Besides—it wasn't like she was planning to stay at Witchery U forever. She would stay just until she and Professor Hottie had figured out who was trying to hurt the chosen ones.

The power of her patron Goddess, Morgana the Red, rose in her as she stared them down.

"Would you just rather I incarcerate the entire Council of Witches for the next fifty years until the children come of age and can protect themselves? It is within my jurisdiction to lock up all of you to protect those girls."

The entire assembly of Council members went silent and blinked at her. It was a delicious moment. She wrinkled her forehead and tilted her chin up as she pretended deep thought.

"Of course, I wouldn't turn any Council member into a toad. That would preclude torturing each member until my warlocks and I can determine who the would-be murderer is," she added.

The murmuring got louder as those around the speaker tugged on his matching butt ugly robe. She struggled not to smirk. He nodded to his cohorts and looked back to her.

"We concede your plan is better," Head Councilman admitted.

Her arms uncrossed and fell to her sides. Her pleased smile swept the crowd.

"Good. Now that's settled, you can all start thinking about how best to determine who among you is trying to kill my successors. You might want to warn him or her that I'm very, very unhappy with this disruption of the hard-won peace I've given more than three hundred years of my life to making happen. When I find the betrayer, he or she will die. If the dragons don't kill him or her first."

"*Dragons? What dragons?*" the Head Councilman demanded.

"The headmaster of Witchery U has dragon guardians hiding among the faculty and staff. Dragons live for thousands of years. They don't want the status quo among magicals to change. My complaint is that their help is a bit heavy handed. They've already ashed an attempted assassin without bothering to find out who in Morgana's name sent him. Why else would I want to get involved? The dragons can fend off assailants all day long. I want to find the source and get rid of the problem."

There was another round of worried grumbling. The Head Councilman held up his hand to silence it.

"Knowing dragons are involved, your plan to oversee the children's training makes a lot more sense. You are the most well-suited witch for such as task."

Jezibaba nodded. "Yes. I'm the only witch living who's immune to dragon fire. The chosen ones could get accidently cooked if they get in the middle of a bunch of warrior dragons trying to kill a single vampire assassin in bat form. Protectors have been appointed, but those connections have not yet been tested."

"Fine. Dragons being involved elevates this matter to one requiring your intervention. Go with our blessing then, Oh Great One," the Head Councilman said.

She nearly sighed when she saw the entire table of heads finally nodding. They lifted their hands and she felt magical approval directed her way. However, she knew a traitor was still among those staring at her.

More than ready to take her leave, Jezibaba raised her hands to bestow her blessing.

"May the Goddess continue

her watch over thee.

As I will this day,

so mote it be."

"*So mote it be,*" they all echoed in reply.

Turning Jezibaba saw Nathaniel's gaze remained on the table of thirteen Council members. He watched a few more seconds, then turned to follow her out of the room. Wards within the room prevented taking their immediate leave. They would have to do so from outside the building.

As they exited, she made a mental note to ask Nathaniel later what he had seen in their energy that had caused such a strange look on his face.

Book Lists (in correct reading order)

HOT DAMNED SERIES

Fashionably Dead
Fashionably Dead Down Under
Hell on Heels
Fashionably Dead in Diapers
A Fashionably Dead Christmas
Fashionably Hotter Than Hell
Fashionably Dead and Wed

SHIFT HAPPENS SERIES

Ready to Were
Some Were in Time
No Were To Run

MAGIC AND MAYHEM SERIES

Switching Hour
Witch Glitch
A Witch in Time
Magically Delicious

HANDCUFFS AND HAPPILY EVER AFTERS SERIES

How Hard Can it Be?
Size Matters
Cop a Feel

If after reading all the above you are still wanting more adventure and zany fun, read *Pirate Dave and His Randy Adventures*, the romance novel budding novelist Rena was helping wicked Evangeline write in *How Hard Can It Be*?

Warning: Pirate Dave Contains Romance Satire, Spoofing, and Pirates with Two Pork Swords.

About Robyn Peterman

Robyn Peterman writes because the people inside her head won't leave her alone until she gives them life on paper.

Her addictions include laughing really hard with friends, shoes (the expensive kind), Target, Coke Zero Cherry with extra ice in a Styrofoam cup, bejeweled reading glasses, her kids, her super-hot hubby and collecting stray animals.

A former professional actress with Broadway, film and T.V. credits, she now lives in the South with her family and too many animals to count.

Writing gives her peace and makes her whole, plus having a job where you can work in your underpants works really well for her. You can leave Robyn a message via the Contact Page and she'll get back to you as soon as her bizarre life permits! She loves to hear from her fans!

Visit **www.robynpeterman.com** for more information.

45077441R00125

Made in the USA
Middletown, DE
13 May 2019